CORE CORRUPTION

Core Calamity Series Book 1

Josef Peeters

Edited by:

Sarah Farrugia
HEARTT Writing & Editing
cosmo12@bigpond.com

Cover Design By: Ashley Redbird

http://redbird-designs.blogspot.com

ISBN-13: 9780645028867

Books by the author

Fiction:
Dumped (psych. drama)
Daintree Denizens (thriller)
Mt. Moulamein (sci-fi)
Transience (magic realism)
Black Heart (psych. thriller)
Endure (dystopian)
THE END (dystopian)
Author's Collection (psyche drama)
Horror Series:
Eat What You Kill (Book 1)
B.A.M. (Book 2)
Eye For An Eye (Book 3)
The Guardians (Book 4) Out soon
BAM Detective Agency Box Set (Books 1-4)

Non-Fiction:
Wood Whisperer Volume 1
Wood Whisperer Volume 2
Wood Whisperer Volume 3
Wood Whisperer Box Set Vol 1-3
Giving Up (Short, autobiographical)

Josef's website with purchasing links;
https://lakesidecaravanpark.wixsite.com/josef

ACKNOWLEDGMENTS

Without readers, an author's words are truly lost, as if they never existed. I salute the readers and the many kind souls who have left glowing reviews of my books. Please know that you are truly appreciated by this humble author.

ONE

"Bitch!"

Although the insult wasn't meant to be heard, it registered clearly in the ears of Dr Rachelle Rizzoli as she leaned heavily on her crutches to move over the metal floor. The awkward movement of her bent and twisted legs encased within the metal braces caused the class of mature students behind her to titter softly. The sound of metal on metal echoed cruelly. When Rachelle reached her desk at the front of the class she turned her ruined visage to the disrespectful students, some of them cringing with the ugliness and horror of it.

"Damn right I'm a bitch. I've earned that title and more by living through more shit than you young pukes are ever likely to realise. You can now add the second and third chapter of your history books to your homework for tonight."

The chorus of groans was met with a steely glare and a raised eyebrow from Rachelle's remaining eye.

"Care to try for chapter four as well?" Met with silence, she continued, "Okay then. Which one of you losers can tell me something you've learned from chapter one?"

"Miss?"

"That would be Doctor Rizzoli to you, Mister Bradley. That was something else I earned. And just as well for you lot. None of us would be alive today if I hadn't earned that PhD."

"That's why she's nothing but a school teacher now," said a voice softly in the back row, which set the other students to smirking and tittering again.

Rachelle slammed her aluminium crutch onto the wooden desk startling the class of twenty students.

"Turn to page 220 in the book, middle of chapter ten. NOW!" she yelled. "Mister Bradley, start reading from the third paragraph. Obviously, none of you bright sparks took the time to read ahead of your class assignments, otherwise, you wouldn't be making stupid remarks. Read, Mister Bradley, if you're capable of performing that onerous task?"

"Despite being labelled a pariah, a maverick, and branded as a

4

criminal, were it not for the heroic and selfless acts of Doctor Rachelle Rizzoli, a geo-physicist employed by the government of the day, Under-City Australis would not have been achievable."

Ken Bradley peered up from the pages of his history book in awe at the bent and broken woman sitting at her desk before him. He would never have guessed in a million years that she was anything but his bitter, mediocre teacher of history.

"Please continue, Mister Bradley," Rachelle insisted in her gravelly voice.

"The-the power necessary to accommodate the survivors of the cataclysm in Australia, once housed underground in the emergency bunker named Under-City Australis by the governing body of directors, would not have been possible had Dr Rizzoli not broken the law by perfecting the device known to have caused the cataclysm in 2150.

"Dr Rizzoli began her experiments in 2153, two years after the bunker was announced and construction began. Racing against time, which scientists estimated to be a mere five years after the event before all life on the surface of the globe would be deemed uninhabitable, Dr Rizzoli managed to single-handedly procure the geo-thermal energy required to service the massive undertaking.

"Later denounced, arrested and tried for crimes of treason, Dr Rizzoli escaped sentencing only by her continued accomplishments benefitting the sole survivors for many generations to come. It is unknown at the time of publication for this book whether Dr Rizzoli enjoys her freedoms or has paid the ultimate price for her selfless actions."

The stunned classroom remained perfectly silent as Ken Bradley finished his reading. Rachelle surveyed the students with contempt, feeling not the least way smug or proud of her continued work. She felt a little ashamed that she had stooped so low as to have to prove herself to the dimwits in front of her. She didn't care what they thought of her. She didn't care what anyone but her biological children thought of her.

"Miss..."

Rachelle glared at the young girl with a fire that threatened to turn her to ash where she sat.

"Doctor Rizzoli," Claire corrected herself, "is it true?"

"Is what true? To which part of the passage are you referring?"

"Did you really use the doomsday device?"

"Good grief! I wish you ignorant lot would stop referring to it as that. It was just a laser drill. A laser drill, which was calibrated incorrectly. The intensity equation used by the eminent Dr Thoms was flawed. That was it. Nothing mysterious and onerous about it. No need for the dramatic label applied to it or him."

"It caused the end of the world," Ken Bradley objected.

"So, none of you exist right now? We are all what? Living a dream, experiencing some form of limbo between existential planes?" Rachelle snorted through her damaged, misshapen nose.

"Well, it caused the end of the life we knew."

"This is the only life you've known, Mister Bradley. Under-City Australis is the sum of your experiences, hardly making you an expert on anything topside. Can anyone tell me what the circumstances topside were like before the cataclysm? Anyone? No? Well, let me tell you, it was no bloody picnic, that's for sure. By the end of the twenty-first century, the world was in turmoil. Natural resources were exhausted, pollution was at an all-time high. New diseases spawned. Health complications soared.

"Energy was at a premium and the governments of every country were ruing the day they privatised their power grids. The crippling costs of energy imposed by the consortiums ruling the power were bringing countries to their knees financially. When I joined the Department of Energy in 2145 to head up their research into commercial geo-thermal energy production, Australia was practically going broke just to pay for basic power to homes and businesses across the continent.

"Australia was at the forefront of initiatives to harvest natural and 'green' sources of energy after a long era of apathy in that direction. Carbon neutrality was a catch-phrase that held little to no influence on the governments of the day. It was too little too late by the time they came around to understanding the consequences of global warming and pollution.

"Dr Thoms understood the need to find an indefinite source of reliable energy. Solar farming only went so far with battery farms unable to be produced through a lack of core elements, namely lithium, for use in lithium-ion batteries. Wind power was insufficient to provide the energy requirements. Wave power and every other form of power generation would not hold a candle to the type of power that geo-thermal energy could sustain. Tapping into that proved difficult and that's where Doctor Thoms demonstrated his mettle. He alone found a way to drill deep enough to access those geo-thermal pockets many kilometres below the surface," Rachelle finished.

"Iceland had sustainable geo-thermal energy long before that, nearly a century before," interrupted Irene Stubble from the back of the room where she held court most days as Class Queen.

Rachelle studied the short-haired girl with so many piercings she couldn't begin to count them, tattoos covering every available skin surface visible, and a multitude of different colours through the spiked coiffure. Regardless of the brat's appearance, Rachelle knew that the girl had brains but seldom used them.

"Someone with something intelligent to add at last. Thank you for joining the class after being silent for a year, Miss Stubble. Yes, Iceland had success with geo-thermal energy because the pockets they accessed were relatively close to the surface. So close that Iceland had many geo-thermal pools where people swam during the coldest months. Two major tectonic plates meet under the island, making it a hot spot for volcanoes providing the flowing magma with which to run the steam turbines that produced 60 - 70% of Iceland's power.

"The geo-thermal pockets beneath our continent were practically unreachable until Dr Thoms produced his laser drill. He began his experiments in the Bougainville trench from a deep-sea platform, to get closer to the source. Can anyone tell me why the location for his experiments was a bad decision?"

"Because of the Pacific Ring of Fire," explained Irene.

"Well, well, well, you never cease to amaze me, young lady. She's correct. Dr Thoms and his research team were literally playing with fire by conducting their experiments so close to one of the most volatile areas on the planet. The Pacific Ring of Fire, so named for the many active and dormant volcanoes creating a horseshoe-shaped 'ring' encompassing many continents and Pacific islands. The ring of fire is a direct result of lithospheric plates colliding to form between 850 - 1000 volcanoes. Four of the largest volcanic eruptions over the last 12,000 years have occurred in the ring of fire.

"Coupled with the incorrect calibration of his drilling device and the known volatility of the location, is what caused the cataclysm which will see the end of life on the surface of the globe within your lifetimes if it hasn't happened already. No one has been able to access the surface for many years now. We have no way of knowing what the present conditions are. The volcanic eruptions continue, that much we know through seismic recordings. The volcanoes continue to spew their lethal mixture of toxic clouds into our atmosphere up there, blocking the sunlight and causing the extinction of all animal life. That's why we're down here and that's why we have to stay down here."

"Not for long," someone voiced.

"No. Not for long. We need air to survive and we're running out of it. The purifiers have been working to keep us alive since 2155 but they're failing. It's estimated we will no longer have breathable air in our city beyond the year 2170, five years from now. The power to run the purifiers and everything else in Under-City Australis is guaranteed, thanks to my efforts, but power isn't all we need to survive, is it? Food! We manage to grow fruit and vegetables in our underground farms and keep basic livestock. Getting rid of the CO_2 we exhale is taken care of, but creating clean air is becoming increasingly difficult and the corrosive effects of the atmosphere are reducing our purifiers' capabilities and their effectiveness. You're all dying and are yet to fully comprehend that fact. You're all so..."

"Attention! Dr Rizzoli, report to the council of directors immediately," the tinny announcement sliced through Rachelle's words.

"Well, aren't you all lucky? Early class dismissal. Make sure you read those chapters tonight ladies and gentlemen, I will be quizzing you on them tomorrow.

Rachelle smiled evilly as she heard the class moan and groan about the homework requirement. The students began the noisy process of gathering their belongings to make the journey through the steel labyrinth to their assigned levels. Rachelle welcomed the break from the rest of the lesson not scheduled to end for another hour normally. She waited until all the smelly students reeking of body odour and ineffective deodorants had vacated before making any moves to rise. The tiresome chore of lifting her mangled body with her aluminium crutches to a standing position was not a sight she wished her students to witness. The ungainly procedure, while quite painful, would only cause snickers and whispered comments.

Sighing with impatience and frustration, Rachelle lumbered awkwardly to her feet, straining with the effort. Making her way along the metal corridors between classrooms caused all manner of grunts and groans to escape between laboured breaths. The noisy clatter of her crutches on the bare metal walkways resounded off the walls next to her.

Level twenty-four, orange section, where Rachelle resided, was a laborious climb down twenty floors from her present level. It would have been just a matter of hopping into one of the freight elevators at either end of the circular walkway around the open central hub, but Rachelle being Rachelle would make the trek down the stairwells next to the elevators no matter how long it took or how painful it became. It was a ritual penance of sorts, carried out each day to remind herself of the mistake she made. The one simple mistake that cost her everything.

Some might take that mistake as being her involvement with Doctor Henry Thoms' laser drill after it was outlawed. Those people would be very wrong. *That* mistake, if one could call it that, resulted in unlimited energy, affording Australia a continuation of life, albeit in greatly reduced numbers, underground. No, her greatest mistake of all happened before that...way before that. It was normally too painful to think about, so Rachelle generally began swearing to herself whenever she started thinking along those lines. One of the reasons for her well-deserved reputation was that she was often seen and heard swearing alone.

The administration level, God's country, white section, was on level one, approximately a kilometre under the surface. It would have been less strenuous for Rachelle to rise to level one than to return to her domicile in orange. Naturally, Rachelle opted to descend to orange. The council of directors would be waiting for clean air topside before Rachelle Rizzoli acquiesced to any of their requests or demands.

Standing before the entrance to the stairwell stood Conrad Boyle with his meaty arms folded resolutely across his massive chest. Conrad Boyle, or Puss-boil, to everyone else due to his acute acne, barred the path Rachelle intended to take. Everything about Boyle set Rachelle's teeth on edge. A razor-sharp flattop buzz cut of his pure white hair, sat above a face made of granite with a ridiculous store-bought tan barely concealing the pock-marks and active zits, giving him ghostly pale skin around the eyes outlining the covers he wore while in the sunbed. Rachelle made a private bet that he didn't sport any tan lines around his groin. The contempt she felt for Boyle did not escape him as she neared.

"Lose your way, Mr Boyle? Thought this level was beneath you?"

"It is," he replied with a comically enquiring frown, not getting the joke.

"Out of my way."

"I'm here to escort you up."

"Wasted trip then. Not going up. I live down. Way down on level twenty-four, orange..."

"I know where you live. I have orders to..."

"If you don't get out of the way I'm going to start screaming rape and blowing my whistle."

Boyle was startled by that threat. Every female in Under-City Australis was equipped with a whistle that, when blown, would ensure that everyone in the vicinity would drop whatever they were doing to attend the emergency. It was one of the hard and fast rules of the city to protect its female population. Any male caught inflicting harm on a female would find themselves facing onerous charges with horrific penalties. Any man found guilty of first-degree rape faced certain castration. Lesser offences met with hard labour around the steam turbines on the basement levels, often a life sentence.

Of course, the whole thing was absurd in Boyle's case but no one else was to know that, especially without the benefit of witnesses. Boyle searched the immediate area. They were alone of course, considering that only the foolhardy would opt to take the stairs. Boyle found himself sweating profusely due to the threat by the annoying, ghastly woman before him.

He felt nothing but disgust for the broken and bitter thing getting about on crutches. There was nothing about her that wasn't repairable nowadays. Huge advances in medicine and surgical procedures, including new limbs and bionic prosthetics, would see the doctor regaining 90% of her mobility and sight. Instead, the ugly woman chose to continue with her ungainly presence through Under-City Australis causing a commotion wherever she went.

Boyle decided, wisely, not to insist on his instructions. While the accusations were laughable, he would be made to endure the painstaking process of having to prove his innocence in a public court. Director Shadforth, to whom he was a personal assistant, would not be amused about seeing his employee in court. He turned smartly on his heel, as though he were some sort of soldier, to make his ignominious exit in the direction of the elevators.

Rachelle continued to her destination with a knowing smirk plastered on her face. Admittedly, her curiosity gnawed at her as she made her way down the stairs, causing quite a racket with her aluminium leg braces and crutches clattering against the steps and railings. The pain began only a few steps down. A deep-seated ache permeated her legs and travelled to her lower back. Sweat formed in the armpits as the awkward movements forced her to endure more hardships the longer she descended.

By the time Rachelle reached orange level, she was swimming in perspiration. Upon entering her domicile through the narrow hatch, she was immediately relieved by the cooler air in her quarters. The living domiciles on orange level were utilitarian with the bare fundamentals for existence. No plush interiors in these parts. Two bedrooms, one combination living/dining/kitchenette area, and one bathroom that would not allow the swinging of a cat, dead or alive.

Her children, both adults now and still on their respective work rosters, occupied one bedroom while she had the other. The thing that depressed Rachelle more than anything about the living conditions was the need for everything to be painted in ghastly orange hues. It wasn't bad enough that the entire ring outside was painted in the garish orange, that it had to extend indoors made it an eyesore to be needlessly tolerated every day.

Once Rachelle had performed the laborious task of undressing, showering for the allotted three minutes and dressed again, she was more exhausted than when she began. Without the leg braces and crutches, she manoeuvred her twisted body into the kitchenette using the handrails placed all around the walls specifically for her assistance, much to the chagrin of the council of directors.

A chime from the central communications hub located in the kitchenette alerted Rachelle to an incoming message.

"Read message," she directed the central computer.

"Message begins," stated the metallic female voice, "Director Shadforth requests an invitation to attend your quarters for an urgent meeting. End message."

"Reply message. Get fucked!"

"Could you repeat the reply, please?" instructed the disembodied voice in a neutral tone.

Rachelle sighed, knowing the message would not reach the ears of the director because of all the filters employed by the software. She supposed that it was a huge compromise on Shadforth's part to make it a request and not a demand. It would have been well within his rights to do so. The council of directors, headed by Karl Shadforth had supreme command and control over all of Under-City Australis and her inhabitants.

"Reply message. If the overlord and deity of white level deems to lower his standards by harkening my door, then permission is granted for a meeting once a meal has been taken."

"Could you repeat the reply, please?"

"Damn it! Can't you just tell him what I want?"

"Please repeat the reply?"

"FUCK! Reply message. Attendance invited for ten o'clock this evening."

"Message sent. Will that be all?"

"Yeah, fuck off you traitor."

"Will that be all?"

"Yes!" replied Rachelle with a frustrated yell and a fist against the steel table fixed to the floor in the centre of the room.

TWO

Gabrielle Rizzoli and Lorenzo Rizzoli each sat at the small table with their mother; a weighty silence hanging between them. Lorenzo (Loz) peered at his older sister, waiting for her to mention it, dying with curiosity to know what the meeting was all about. Gabrielle (Gabs) simply munched on the bland meal with a bored expression giving away none of the emotion behind the pretty face framed by long dark tresses.

Rachelle was pushing her food around the plate waiting for one of her children to break the ice with the obvious question once she announced the pending visitation from 'heaven'. The unconcerned look on the face of her daughter failed to mask the anxiety she knew was lurking beneath the surface. Rachelle smiled inwardly at the dress and demeanour of her children. Even before the announcement about the meeting was revealed, her children had showered and dressed for the occasion in their best and cleanest clothes.

Loz especially smelled clean and fresh despite his ten-hour shift in the bowels of the city tending to the natural waste of the inhabitants. His profession as a junior sanitation engineer saw him returning from his gruelling shifts reeking like he had taken a swim in the sewage ponds. Rachelle had warned him about a million times to undress outside the domicile before entering. It was her lot to gather his reeking clothing in a plastic bag afterwards, which she would throw straight into the washer with a ton of deodorising detergent thrown in. His clothes continued to smell regardless of the treatments.

"How come you knew?" growled Rachelle suddenly, startling the pair.

Gabs peered at her mother through the fringe of glossy black hair, shampooed to within an inch of its life. Remarkable really, considering the precious few minutes allotted to each member of the domicile.

"Director Shadforth showed up at work today to ask me why you ignored his request for a meeting on white level."

"And what did you answer?"

"I told him that Earth would have to turn sunny again before you deigned to venture upland." replied Gabs.

"Clever girl. You know your mother well. Shithead sent his Puss-boil to fetch me. Not sure who I detest more of the two."

"Go on and tell him that, why don't you?" Gabs dared.

"You think I haven't already? Seems you don't know me at all in that case. So, Shadforth showed up on green level where you work? Don't tell me he went to see you in the bowels on black level, Loz?"

"Nah, sis told me," admitted Loz with a smirk.

"Is that all that was said, Gabs?"

"N-nooo..."

"Well, that was a drawn-out no, if ever I've heard one. Sounds ominous. Go on. Spit it out."

"Nothing much," replied Gabs attempting to sound nonchalant.

It didn't work with her mother who grew ever more suspicious the more hesitant her daughter became. Unfortunately, she wasn't able to read Gabs as well as she could her son. When her son tried to avoid conversation, it was always clear what he was hiding. It was as if Rachelle could read his brainwaves. Her daughter was far too similar in temperament and nature to Rachelle. She had never been able to read Gabs the same way. However, she knew something of major concern or importance was behind Gabs' hesitancy.

"Gabs?"

"Hmmm?"

"Something you need to tell me?"

"Just..." she began to say and stopped sharply.

"Damn! Must be worse than I thought. Now you *have* to tell me," Rachelle ordered.

"Well, he hinted at things more than coming right out with anything."

"Such as?" Rachelle asked in a cold, hard voice, which her children knew preceded a doomsday eruption.

"Mum..."

"Get on with it," Rachelle demanded in a death-rattle whisper.

"I-I got the impression...that there would be reprisals for us if you refused to meet with him," Gabs finally admitted with moisture collecting on her brow.

Loz cringed with the expectation of a tyrannical tide. She

surprised him...

"He said that to you?"

"Not in so many words, no. I-I was reading between the lines. Please don't get me in trouble again with my boss or the Director, Mum. Last time I was demoted to shit-kicker, literally. Carting shit around for months to fertilise the plants."

"So, the coward didn't come right out with it, he left it to you to gather the meaning of his double-speak? He threatened you and Loz with repercussions if I didn't play ball with him, eh? Oh, this is going to be a fun meeting. I'm looking forward to this one."

"Mum, you promised," insisted Gabs.

"I promised nothing. Want me to ask the system for a playback?"

"Please, Mum. I love what I do as a botanist. I don't want to go down any levels from that."

"Careful, young lady, we *live* lower than that level," Rachelle warned with a steely tone, her face twisting more than was usual.

"You know that's not what I meant."

"Do I? Your sense of superiority hasn't escaped our attention of late."

Gabs straightened her posture at the accusation. Only, when she looked to her brother for support, he grimaced and shrugged and nodded his head in affirmation of his mother's assessment.

"I see. Let the real shit-kicker please stand up."

"Watch yourself, young lady. Loz *applied* for his job and worked damn hard at his lessons to make the grades."

"Meaning I didn't?"

"Take it to mean what you want."

"That isn't fair. I worked just as hard as anyone to get where I am."

"Working hard at kissing arse compared to what this family does, are two very different scenarios."

"And exactly whose arse am I supposed to be kissing?"

"Who came to see you today? When was the last time anyone else saw that prick below white? After what he did to me, to us, and you still brown-nose to him? You'll regret it one day, believe me. Karl Shadforth uses whomever he wishes then casts them aside or demotes them to lower and lower levels until they're never seen or heard from again. Why do you think we live on orange?"

"You," she spat. "You're the sole reason we live on this disgusting level. You and your high and mighty attitudes. You and your meddling with illegal instruments of death. You and your horrible face and body. You're a freak, just like they say, and a crap mother. Daddy would..."

The slap stung more than Gabs could say. She knew she'd gone a step too far, even as she voiced it. She also conceded that she was wrong for thinking it. Her father couldn't have provided any better for them. They wouldn't have survived the cataclysm if it weren't for their mother unless they just happened to be one of the lucky lottery winners awarded entry to Under-City Australis. It was her mother's involvement and procurement of enough steam power to run the city that secured their entry.

Gabs felt a pang of guilt at that. She remembered her many friends who remained aloft. They would all have died a horrible death after a sustained period of hardship, choking on the toxic atmosphere, gagging on the dust and soot until their lungs were no longer able to function. Hundreds of active volcanoes in the ring of fire erupting every day, spewing millions of tonnes of ash into the atmosphere, blocking sunlight for years.

The ones who didn't perish immediately from the quakes that rocked the globe, or were immolated by the magma flows, were left to suffer immeasurably by nature and humankind when they turned feral. It always brought a tear to Gabs' eyes when she thought about the folks they left behind.

As far as mentioning her father? That was a subject best left entirely alone. Opening up that can of worms caused nothing but heartache for them all. Though her memories were distant and somewhat coloured by time to be seen in a rosier hue, Gabs knew of the grief and suffering attributable to the man she called her father. One look at what her mother had become was enough to make her regret her words and feel a pang of terrible guilt, no matter how angry she was.

"Sorry, Mum. I really am. That was a horrible thing to say and not true."

Rachelle took a long moment before she found her voice again. The mention of their father caused all manner of devastating images to flow through her mind, especially...the final blow! The ride through Hell and back again for Rachelle. The cause of so much pain and mental anguish that the vivid memory never failed to produce the phantom pains associated with it. A nightmare that ran through her mind every evening, without fail unless Rachelle succumbed to prescribed narcotics. She resorted to the drugs only now and then, to catch up with some sleep. Even the painkillers for all her injuries were only taken once or twice a month, when the pain became unbearable.

"Don't you ever mention that animal again in my presence, let alone that he might somehow be a better alternative for you kids. Look at me!" Rachelle yelled suddenly, startling the pair.

"Look at what he did to me. Remember what he did to you? Do you?"

They both nodded silently.

"Your guests have arrived. Do you wish me to let them in?" asked the house-bot.

"NO! That piece of shit doesn't get to enter my quarters. And Puss-boil can rot for all I care."

"Your guests have arrived."

"I know that you ninny. Fuck your filters. One of these days I'm going to recode you."

"Your guests..."

"Tell my guests to wait and I will be there soon," said Rachelle impatiently, muttering about bloody-minded computers as she struggled to rise from her chair, always a major demand on her ailing body.

Loz ran to retrieve her crutches for her. The clatter of the crutches could be heard ringing on the metal floors as Rachelle made her way to the main entrance. Once the hatch was open, she glared at Karl Shadforth with undisguised venom. Reserving a special look of further disdain for Puss-boil standing right beside his sugar daddy.

"Hello, Rachelle..."

"That would be Doctor Rachelle Rizzoli, or just Doctor Rizzoli, to you," replied Rachelle with a sneer.

"As I am a doctor myself, I thought we could dispense with..."

"Honorary, mate! Not earned like mine. A store-bought degree will not get you my respect or acknowledgement as an equal."

"I see. It is to be a hostile reception then?"

"What do you think? Why would it be anything else,

Shadforth?"

"That would be, Director Shadforth to you. Quid pro quo?"

"You look that one up, did you? What do you want?"

"May we come in?"

"If you must. Not your toady though. That piece of..."

"Watch it," warned Karl with a growing temper.

"Or what? You'll demote me? Make me go down a few more levels? Been there, done that, remember?"

"You can't hold me responsible..."

"Oh, but I can and do. You were the one who lobbied for my hearing, the one who insisted on sentencing even though I was found not guilty of most charges. By rights, my children and I should be on white level with you, but no, here we are. Not that I mind. I prefer to be here than anywhere near you. I'd be just as content on black level so your threats mean nothing to me. Do your worst."

"There are more people to consider than just yourself, though, aren't there?" pushed Karl through his smarmy grin.

Loz and Gabs had hold of an arm each as Rachelle's roar of rage echoed throughout the level causing more than one or two hatches to open. As strong as both children were due to the physicality of their respective jobs, they struggled to restrain their mother. Her attempts to remove Karl Shadforth's head and shit down his throat, such as she was threatening in words, made the man and his lackey back up a step or two.

Once Rachelle had run out of steam, she shrugged off her children, only to stand glaring at Karl.

"I could have you arrested and charged for that," said Karl.

"Figured out the passcode yet?"

"We will. We will."

"Not before it all shuts down at midnight on New Year's Eve, though. So, go ahead and lock me up. You've had your top minds on that conundrum for years and still no progress. I know because I'd be in the shit box if you had."

Karl Shadforth shifted his posture to stare down the ugly woman. As much as he would have loved to do exactly as she suggested, he knew that the result would be catastrophic for UCA. Once power for the city was cut off, it would spell the end for them all. It had been a stalemate between the two combatants since their arrival in the under city.

Karl had indeed championed the efforts to have her sentenced to death, or serve life in the bowels of UCA. The bombshell she revealed before her sentencing hearing in a private room with only him and Rachelle, had forced Karl to back-peddle. Though it irked him no end to capitulate to extortion, he was left with few alternatives. If she was locked up or sentenced to death despite being found not guilty on all but two charges levelled at her, she would not be able to input the passcode on the computer handling all the functions of geothermal input for the immense steam turbines at the end of each year.

UCA would die if that happened. They had attempted to bypass or cut off the main computers on many occasions to no avail. Rachelle held the key to that and the laser drill, which effectively negated the possibility of drilling a new path to the geothermal pocket to eliminate the need for her set-up. They could have shut her operation down and used their own if they knew how to engineer the drill she perfected. All the design specs had been wiped from every Earthly hard drive when it was outlawed. Only Rachelle retained the ability to construct the laser drill and she refused point-blank to repeat it or teach it to anyone after she destroyed the device. She knew what would result if she did.

Karl found himself back-peddling once more where the annoying bitch was concerned. Although the new threat hanging over the city would see them all suffocating within a few short years, it still required her input for the power generation to continue until that time. Cutting off their supply before the end was a fait accompli, simply wasn't an option. Every ounce of time they could squeeze out of the failing purifiers meant another opportunity to find a solution.

Science had leapt ahead during their time underground. Breakthroughs occurred every day in every branch of the sciences. It was for that reason he was visiting the woman's level, as distasteful as it was. The smell below white became more unbearable the lower they went. Orange level was disgusting, putrid! Karl wasn't quite sure how anyone could stand it. Not that he would be diverting any resources to assist in the matter any time soon. Karl squared his shoulders as he came to a decision.

"Dr Rizzoli, you have until noon tomorrow to attend an appointment at my office on white. If you fail to appear, you and your children will be arrested and charged with sedition. There are matters at hand that go well beyond your petty concerns and objections. The fate of UCA and all its inhabitants are at stake. Your present attitude prevents me from outlining the great opportunity I was attempting to offer. A chance to wipe the slate clean and make amends for all humanity."

Karl turned on his heels with Boyle in tow, heading straight to the elevator. He turned to look back at the family one final time with a look of smug satisfaction on his features.

THREE

At precisely 11:59 am the following morning, Rachelle presented herself at the outer office of the Head Director for the Council of Directors in UCA. Sitting at the handsome desk in the expansive and opulent foyer, was none other than Puss-boil dressed in his fancy outfit for the day highlighting every steroid-purchased muscle in his upper body, his glowing tan displaying reverse panda eyes and a mouth full of teeth gleaming in the bright overhead lights. It was obvious to Rachelle that power conservation or economy was unheard of in Heaven.

She stood before the desk without a word, while Puss-boil waited for Rachelle to announce herself. Sighing impatiently when he realised he wasn't about to hear from the rude bitch, he reached over to press the intercom button on the stainless-steel apparatus resting on a corner of the desk. Talking quietly through the headset he wore on one ear, Boyle announced the arrival of Doctor Rizzoli, making sure to get the title right and was able to be heard by the woman before him.

Rachelle rolled her eyes when he nodded his head in acknowledgement of the instructions he received.

"You may go through to Director Shadforth's office," he announced.

"Did he hear you nod?"

"Huh?"

Rachelle ignored the dumb-arse as she proceeded to make her way through the elaborately carved wooden doors. Wrestling herself and her crutches through the opening awkwardly, she made her way, to an even larger and more ornate desk than the one she had just stood at.

"I see you're ready to act professionally and cordially."

The stony silence hung in the air.

"Please have a seat," Karl offered. "Refreshment?"

Silence.

"Rachelle...sorry. Dr Rizzoli, this behaviour is counterintuitive to our joint objectives. I assure you that what I have to offer, the proposal I am about to reveal, will have enormous benefits for us all, especially you. Please have a seat, as this will take some time to explain."

"It is difficult getting in and out of chairs. I'm far more comfortable standing. And no, I don't want a bloody refreshment. I don't want your ridiculous small talk, platitudes, promises or anything else. All I want is an explanation for my presence, so I can reject whatever the proposal is and get back down to my lousy teaching job and my life."

"It didn't have to be like this. You were offered all the medical assistance you required. Your body could have been repaired, even re-built."

"At great cost to me."

"Hardly a cost at all."

"Shadforth, you are about as trustworthy as one of the enormous ground worms we have down here. If I reveal the passcode to you, I will be left to rot in the bowels and no amount of your posturing trying to convince me otherwise will ever make me believe you. I am content with my body the way it is. It's everyone else that has a problem with it and I don't give a rat's arse what everyone else thinks or feels. Are you going to stop wasting my time or not? As much as I prefer to stand as opposed to sitting and then rising again, I'm unable to stand for extended durations."

"Very well. Unfortunately, you remain hostile but I guess that is just because you really are the bitch that everyone keeps labelling you as. You are a miserable pain in my arse, that's for sure."

"I think that job is already taken and I don't have the requisite equipment?"

Rachelle almost laughed as Karl turned beet red and mumbled and fussed with his shirt collar hoping for something clever to say.

"You, you have no idea what you're talking about and I resent the insinuation," said Karl tersely before gathering his emotions neatly.

"Everyone else in UCA knows what I'm talking about, though."

Rachelle smiled evilly as she watched Karl squirm in his plush leather seat.

"You are an extremely unlikeable person. If it weren't for the good of all, I would not be making this offer to you."

"Bit absurd to be coming over as altruistic to me, Shadforth. That's even less believable than anything else you've said. I know you for the narcissistic, egotistical ponce you are. There is nothing you do that doesn't involve some advantage or perk for yourself."

"Rizzoli, you need to...."

"GET ON WITH IT!" Rachelle screamed, remembering his threat from the previous evening, incurring her abject ire once more.

The door to the office flew open as Boyle entered with a look of dread on his features and his body tensed for violence. Karl waved him back with a nod of assurance that all was in hand.

"Very well," Karl said as the door closed. "If you refuse to sit then we may as well perambulate."

"You must have been scouring a dictionary just before I entered to come up with that one. In what fucking universe do you think I am capable of perambulating?"

"You can crab-walk or crawl or whatever else it is you do so very awkwardly, while I walk and we'll talk as we go. I have several eminent scientists I want you to meet. The first will be Doctor Blake Tooth, who has nothing to do with dentistry before you make an inane comment."

Karl did not wait for Rachelle to agree as he minced past her. His manner was so obvious that everyone was aware of his predilections. He passed through a door at the rear of his office that led into an all-white corridor lined with large viewing windows into sterile laboratories on either side. Rachelle struggled to keep up with the man as she peered in wide-eyed wonder at the many white-gowned scientists and medical personnel working diligently behind the panels of hardened Plexiglass. She felt some degree of envy rising within her. Their laboratories were cutting edge.

Karl waved his wristband at a door scanner to gain access into one of the laboratories on the right-hand side. Not bothering with any of the minions along the path to the rear office, Karl strode confidently into the office of Dr Tooth, concealed behind an array of computer monitors.

"Blake."

"Karl," replied the doctor without peering up from his keyboard.

"Blake, this is Doctor Rizzoli. The woman I was telling you about. I would like you to brief her on what we're doing here, namely your invaluable contribution," said Karl as he plonked himself into a chair in front of Blake's desk.

Wheeling himself around from behind his desk on his chair, Blake peered at Rachelle with an unnerving, calculating glare.

"How do you do? Please have a seat?"

"No," she replied. "Get on with it."

"Karl?" he asked in confusion.

"Consider her a hostile volunteer at best and a bloody nuisance at a fraction less than best," Karl replied dismissively.

"I see," said Blake not seeing at all. "Very well then. I am a neurosurgeon and software engineer with degrees from..."

"Spare me your bona fides and the self-congratulatory praise. Cut to the chase. My legs are aching and I need to go home to rest.

"I...what? Oh! Yes, I see. How to be quick? So much to tell. Um, let me see if I can gloss over the salient points. My research was primarily involved with dementia and patients suffering from varying degrees of Alzheimer's. My idea was to accurately map the human brain of a patient before the onset of serious symptoms where memory loss became problematic. Utilising my other speciality of software coding, I then developed a way of digitising that output.

"The idea being, you see, of re-inputting, reinfusing that information into the patient's brain once the disease managed to wipe out the memories."

"Something Blake has succeeded in doing with several volunteers. Due to his success, dementia is almost a thing of the past if we get to map and digitise someone's brain in time."

"Fascinating. Are you alluding to the possibility that I exhibit early symptoms of dementia?"

"No, not at all. On we go to see the next person, a brilliant physicist, George Grover. He's located in the laboratory next door, so not so far to travel, eh?"

Karl rose swiftly from the chair, enjoying the fact that he was able to lord his superior movability over Rachelle. He sashayed through the lab exit and to the next door over, where he waved his wrist at the scanner. He followed a direct path down the centre of the lab to reach another office with an equally stunning array of computers covering every square inch of the desk surface.

"George Grover, this is Doctor Rizzoli."

"This! She? You can't be serious?" said George Grover in a

high-pitched voice.

A true pin-head if ever there was one. Balding at the front of his very pointy head, with a halo of unruly locks. A proboscis that a rhino would be proud of, perched squarely in the centre of his face. Beneath a pathetic attempt at a moustache, were a pair of thin lips which worked themselves into a veritable lather as he contemplated the mangled woman before him.

"We can't be choosy, George. You know that. Besides, it doesn't make any difference how she looks *now*," said Karl cryptically and almost conspiratorially.

"How much do you want me to reveal?" asked George in his squeaky mouse-like voice.

"Tell her what you've told me and don't get bogged down in all the jargon. I can't bear it when you waffle on in fifteen syllable words that no one understands. Keep it simple. Dumb it down so even ...she can understand," he said waving his hand dismissively in Rachelle's direction.

Rachelle held her tongue and her temper in check for the time being while she tried to get her head around what the heck she was hearing and what it had to do with her.

"Are you familiar with the Einstein-Rosen bridge principle?"

"Essentially folding space-time, creating a wormhole?"

"Close enough. Much about the theory remained just that, a theory for many years. My research into the possibility of creating an artificial Einstein-Rosen bridge was problematic to begin with while topside. Being that space travel was almost a thing of the past. Down here, I believed my research was at an end..."

"Stop trying to build up the tension before you get to your anti-climactic end, George. Get to the gist of the matter, would you?" Karl was becoming impatient.

"Oh dear, oh dear. Okay, okay. Er, where was I? Yes. I did it."

Rachelle stood there with a look of confusion, unsure what had been revealed if anything.

"Did what?" she finally asked.

"Created an artificial bridge."

"You two are a pair of clowns, you know that? Only, I'm not laughing. I have no idea what you're on about or why I'm here and how any of this connects. Perhaps now that your bridge is built you should get over it?"

"Perhaps I might enlighten her?" suggested Karl. To put it in a nutshell, we want to send a data packet to someone."

"Who?"

"You."

"Me?"

"Yes."

"That's called an email where I come from and I didn't need to hear all this shit to be sent one."

"You don't understand."

"Got that right. The first thing anyone has said that's made any sense today."

"Okay, let me try to backtrack without getting too bogged down in the minutiae."

"Ha, ha," chuckled George.

"Did you like what I did there?" asked Karl enjoying his joke.

"I'm going..."

"Hold on, hold on. I'm getting there. George here has discovered a method of producing a miniature wormhole in an artificial vacuum, right here in this laboratory. He doesn't have to go into space to do it. We intend to utilise that technology to send someone through the wormhole."

"A miniature someone?"

"What? No. What are you talking about?"

"You just said that George can only produce a miniature wormhole."

"Well, yes, that's true. You see we wouldn't be sending a whole person through, just the data packet."

"Huh?"

"Oh my, you do seem to be quite dense. I understood it as he explained it. Why can't you?"

"Maybe because you had more background information to go on whereas I'm in the dark."

"We tried to give you the background information but you kept asking us to gloss over it. Can't have it both ways."

"Alright just back it up a bit without going into fine details. George here creates a miniature bridge so that you can send a data package. Where are you going to send it and what is it?"

"Not where...when."

"Sorry? Are we talking time travel?"

"Exactly. Into the past, to be specific. The data package is the digitised brain scan. Look the bridge lasts only milliseconds, is incredibly minuscule and takes an enormous amount of power. We don't have the luxury of grand experiments in attempting to increase the size or longevity of the bridge to try and get living people through. We're inhibited by the time constraints thrust upon us by the failing air purifiers. We need to fix things before humanity is doomed to extinction. We aren't the only Under-City experiencing these failures. Under-City India (UCI), has gone already as far as we know. Under-City Europa (UCE), and Under-Sity America (USA), are in the same fix as we are. Who knows how the rest are faring? We lost communications with many of them when the conditions topside worsened about two years ago."

"Wait a second. You said you were going to send through the digitised brain scan? That's the data package?"

"Yes."

"Who are you going to send it to and how do they receive it? What? You send it to a computer?"

"No. The digitised bran scan is shot through the bridge at the speed of light because it is essentially piggybacked onto a photonic beam. The human brain runs on brain waves, electrical impulses at different frequencies, delta, theta, alpha, beta and gamma, plus one other wave hidden to medical science until now, that separates every living human. A kind of neural fingerprint, if you will. It is that precise frequency and oscillation pattern that allows us to reinfuse a healthy data package into an ailing one. Only the original host can accept the infusion which manifests itself almost instantaneously. Only something microscopic will fit through the wormhole at this point. Blake Tooth has successfully implanted the digitised brain scans by passing the beam directly through the patient's heads, here in UCA, which recognises and absorbs its zeta waves, leaving them with a normal, healthy intellect afterwards."

"And the point of sending a brain into the past is? I can't believe I'm asking this question or having this conversation, by the way."

"To undo the past. To prevent the cataclysm."

"You do realise you're dealing with immense paradoxes if you start down that road? Theoretically, that is, because it isn't possible."

"We're a little beyond theory at this point. Quite a bit more advanced, actually."

"Yet here we are, with all life about to be extinguished...still."

"That's because we haven't tried to alter anything yet."

"Hold on. Are you saying you've already done it? Sent someone's brain back in time?"

George was getting a sore neck bouncing back and forth between the pair. He had tried to intervene on several occasions unsuccessfully. In the end, he gave up and looked down, peeved that Karl was stealing his thunder. George was very proud of his achievements.

"Correct."

"Whose?"

"That is highly classified."

"Well, why haven't they changed things then? Why are we still in this shithole?"

"Because we have to find and utilise exactly the right person with access to certain people. The other most important information we require of the recipient is their exact location in three-dimensional space and time. We have to have precise coordinates for the transfer to take place. The amount of mathematics that goes into the physics of the thing is astronomical. But none of that matters if we can't send someone back with the right connections and the wherewithal to make a difference."

"And you have someone like that?"

"We do."

"Who?"

"You."

FOUR

The laughter erupting from Rachelle could be heard throughout the lab. Karl rushed to close the office door. He smoothed down his ultra-white suit jacket unnecessarily before resuming his seat. He and George waited impatiently for the madwoman to stop her insane cackling.

"Finished?" asked Karl with a steely edge when Rachelle finally ceased.

"You're even stupider than I thought you were. You're also wasting my bloody time. I have classes this afternoon..."

"Your classes have been reassigned. Your employment has been terminated. Your children have been placed on extended leave without privileges. You will be forced to move to black where you will live the few years left to us all in that hell hole if you refuse to cooperate," Karl ended with smug satisfaction.

The blow struck him cleanly on the chin, successfully removing several teeth and breaking his jaw in the process. The metal crutch then swung the other way to connect with George in much the same manner, effectively knocking him unconscious. Karl struggled on the floor with blood spraying from his ruined nose, saturating his pristine white suit, while moaning and clutching his broken jaw. Rachelle moved herself to hover over the stricken man. After having removed the rubber stopper from the bottom of the crutch, Rachelle placed the tip firmly onto Karl's neck. She applied pressure with the sharp, exposed end.

"You need to listen very carefully to me now. No man will ever again threaten me or my children. I made that promise to myself after the creature that did this to me. I will kill you and this jerk-off here if you ever so much as look at me the wrong way. Do you understand me, you mealy little cockroach?"

Karl's eyes almost bulged from their sockets. Fear coursed through his system. His face ached. His nose and jaw were a ruin. Reconstructive surgery was a certainty. Even though death stared him in the face, his worst fears were for the damage done to his face, his rugged good looks, as he saw himself. Karl was unaware that everyone else saw him as a pasty-faced, effeminate fool except for his toady.

Rachelle had banked on the fact that Puss-boil would not be accompanying them on their little tour, figuring he didn't have the necessary security clearances. She waited for the opportunity to act out her plan, one that she had concocted the moment the prick had threatened her children the previous evening. She could play-act at anything to gain his confidence when it came to the safety of her children. Hadn't she already proven that? Her broken body was testament to the fact.

Karl and his cronies should have understood, should have researched her history more closely before making threats. They had chosen completely the wrong target for their scheme. Rachelle crossed over that particular bridge a long time ago with a man capable of worse than Karl represented. She fought that person and won...to a degree, and she would win the next round with her new adversary as well. She removed a piece of paper from her inner coat pocket while keeping up the pressure on his windpipe.

"On this contract, Shadforth, are your instructions that my children are never again to be held liable for anything in Under-City Australis or anywhere else. They are never to have their privileges or employment removed, revoked, replaced or interfered with unless voluntarily requested by them in front of impartial witnesses. I will be retired from active duty as a teacher with full benefits for life, or when natural events like loss of breathable air cuts that term short. You will sign this, and your friend here will witness it and you will never again threaten me or have anything to do with me. Understand?"

Karl began to shake his head in the negative until the pressure on the crutch tip increased, blocking his air intake. By the time he began to turn a shade of blue, he was nodding as best he was able with the restrictive impediment on his neck.

"The paper has the appropriate insert to take your wrist input and George's. You don't even have to physically sign it. Give it your approval, now," she whispered.

Karl waved his wrist at the paper. When the signal beep from the wrist implant confirmed his approval, Rachelle removed the crutch from his neck. George was gradually coming out of it as she made her way to him. She grabbed his wrist roughly after bending down precariously. She waved his wristband over the paper in the same fashion until she heard the tell-tale beep.

"You, you don't understand, Rachelle," George muttered as he rose from the floor slowly. "Your, your children...everyone, dead. It hasn't been made public yet. Poison."

"Are you trying to imply that you've poisoned my children?"

"N-no. Everyone is slowly dying and much sooner than expected. While, while the purifiers may work for a few more years the decrease in their efficiency is allowing toxic elements to enter our city. Everyone will succumb within a few short months, six at the most. You were our Hail Mary. The only person remaining on the planet with the type of access and other criteria to make it happen, to reverse it. To save not only your children and yourself, but everyone on the planet," admitted George getting stronger, recovering from the blow, albeit with a lump forming on his brow and the makings of a class one headache building.

"So, you're lying to the populace, keeping up the pretence of a few years left to what, prevent riots?"

"Something like that. You saw what happened topside, or at least the beginning of it after the lottery winners were announced? What will happen down here when we tell them they have months to live?"

"Why me?"

"Your relationship with Thoms."

"I didn't have a 'relationship' with Dr Thoms and why would it be an advantage if it was true?"

"You knew him, you studied under him and..."

"And?"

"He, he...had a thing for you according to our sources."

"Bullshit!"

"We have a recording of him speaking to one of his colleagues about how he felt. Only he couldn't act on his feelings because of the student-teacher relationship. He was bound by ethics and respect not to act on his impulses."

"You made secret recordings of my old tutor? That's..."

"Necessary, as it turned out."

"You make it sound like spying on him led you to some sort of result. I know that isn't true because, well, here we are. Had you good reason to spy on Dr Thoms and found out about his blunder before it happened then nothing would have prevented you from putting an end to his experiments. I don't believe you. The point is moot."

At Rachelle's feet, Karl began mumbling and moaning, ostensibly demanding to be allowed to seek medical help, or calling for his mummy. Rachelle couldn't be sure which. She poked him sharply with her crutch in the ribs to quiet him down. He moaned even louder. She poised the crutch above his face with a glare, which had the desired effect.

"Okay, give it to me straight, then. What was your plan involving me? How did you see it playing out?"

"We know where you were at a precise point in time and space. We can input those spatial coordinates into the computer banks with pinpoint accuracy. We have very little leeway for error. We're talking micro millimetres. If we are as much as the tiniest percentage out with our calculations, the photon beam would miss the target. A bit like trying to shoot a single microbe in the ocean. The computations are not only about earthly three-dimensional coordinates but time as well. The calculations required for the transference across time takes days for the most advanced computers we have. Days, we are running short on."

"Tell me the procedure," she asked.

"Um, shouldn't we do something to help...?"

"Eventually. Let him suffer for the moment. Give him time to reflect on his behaviour to prevent him from going around threatening people. He'll be as good as new after they've finished with him," replied Rachelle dismissively. Karl's eyes bugged out even more.

"First step is to make a complete scan of your brain and the associated wave patterns, especially the new one we are calling the Zeta Wave. It's that particular wave that makes everything possible. It is unique to every individual and the reason the infusion works. The photon beam with the digitised insert is set to mimic the exact frequency and oscillation pattern of the Zeta Wave. Once it passes through the host's brain, it is immediately adopted and immersed into the brain, taking over completely with a new set of instructions, memories and experiences. Well, in your case. In our dementia patients, we were only giving them old memories."

"Meaning?"

"A full invasive scan isn't required for our dementia patients.

Yours would be complete and very invasive. Your scan would be entering your younger self, one without your current experiences. How many folks have dreamed of starting over at the prime of their life, only, knowing everything they know when they reach a more mature age? You are being offered the opportunity of a lifetime, a chance to become whole again with all the knowledge you have at present, all those skills."

"Hold on. What are you talking about? *When*, are we talking about?"

"Your employment interview with the Department of Energy. We know your precise location at a given time. It was previously recorded on CCTV footage. We know everything about the office where the interview took place. The height of the chair, its position in relation to the desk where you were sitting, everything. As I said, we need pinpoint accuracy to get it right. There is no margin for error."

"What happens to me?"

"Umm...you mean here after we do your scan?"

"Of course, I meant here. What happens to my life here while the younger me is figuring out ways of saving the world? Wow! Never thought that was a line I'd ever be using."

"Hmm."

"I don't think I'm going to like the answer to that, am I?"

"The type of scan we have to do on a time transferee is...exceptional. Unlike our dementia patients who only have to have their memories restored, a time transferee must have a complete...ah...removal."

"Come again?"

"It isn't a copy of some parts of the brain, but a removal of that consciousness and all its functions."

"Are you insane? Why would I even contemplate such a thing?"

"Ask yourself this; why would you need the old body? You, the conscious you, would be alive and well in your younger self. If you succeeded in your mission, your movements would be affecting the outcome of the present. If it were possible for you to remain in two time frames simultaneously, you might be teaching a class one day here and suddenly your arm would break for no apparent reason, following an event that occurred years earlier while your younger self fell off her skis or something. Everything you do when you go back and start living a new life will have present repercussions...for us all. Especially you, though. There is no alternative, in any case."

"So, I'm reduced to a vegetable here?"

"Oh, no. We'd euthanize you, of course."

"WHAT? Now I know you're nuts. What about my children?"

"Well..."

That was when it hit Rachelle like a torpedo to the solar plexus. The sudden revelation caused her to falter precariously, swaying like a drunkard until she collapsed into the chair previously occupied by Karl with a painful thud.

"You...you can't mean it. You can't ask me... No, no, no. That's what you meant when...whole again."

FIVE

Sitting in a daze opposite her children that evening, Rachelle ran through everything that happened, including her final warning to Karl Shadforth as he lay on the cold, white floor, fractured, bleeding red.

Just in case you have any ideas about reneging on our deal or using high-priced legal experts to get out of it, I advise you to remember a certain donation you made just after entering UCA. Do you recall the magnanimous gesture you made toward the future diversity of the gene pool? A friend made sure I have a sample of that locked away in case of anything you dare to scheme, Shadforth. You'll find yourself in court facing execution or castration so quickly your head will spin if I get so much as a whisper that you're trying something. Fancy a life without those little balls you have? No? Well, then, make sure my children and I hear nothing more from you...ever!

The moment of satisfaction she felt after that was short-lived. The enormity of what was being asked of her had hit home with devastating effect, leaving her panting painfully after an anxiety attack on her way back to orange. For the first time since entering UCA, Rachelle used the elevator to return to her level. If she had opted for her usual penance by taking the stairs, she might not have made it at all.

All of white would be talking and gossiping about the raving lunatic screaming her foul-mouthed invective to all and sundry on her prolonged jaunt through the level. Many good folks on white had never heard some of the words used by the madwoman. Everyone steered a wide berth around her should they have had the misfortune of coming across her on their travels.

"Mum?"

Rachelle looked up from her lap to peer at her gorgeous daughter, "Hmm?"

"Are you going to talk about it?"

"About what, Gabs?" replied Rachelle with a hint of impatience and a forlorn hope that her children had no idea what had transpired.

Forlorn hope because nothing was secret in UCA. Word of her antics on white had reached orange before she did. A resident of that level enquired after her in a mock-caring manner as she hobbled past the lady's door. The enquiry was ignored with its usual indifference by the crab-woman of orange. Looked like a crab, walked like a crab; must be a crab! No one could honestly attest to the fact that it might be a female crab. It was an assumption, a guess.

"About your meeting with Direct..."

"Don't you say that name or afford it a title it doesn't deserve. That thing is evil incarnate. I am hoping that I've arranged to have nothing whatever more to do with him or I swear I'll kill him."

"MUM!"

"What? You think I care what happens to me? Look at me, Gabrielle. Look at me."

"You too, Lorenzo. No man alive will ever do this to me or threaten my children again. I will do anything...everything in my power to ensure that I will never be a victim, especially to a man."

"I understand that, Mum, I do. I remember what it was like. I know you think we don't, but you're wrong. We don't like to think about it but we do remember it all. This, though, goes way beyond any one of us. Why wouldn't you do what was being offered?"

"You have no idea what was being asked of me."

"Yes, we do. He told us."

"Really?"

"Not sure why you're so surprised. Of course, he told us. We were both summoned to his office before our shifts began this morning."

"Well, you may know then what was being asked but you fail to consider the dire implications."

"What's so dire about the opportunity to be whole again? No one deserves that more than you," said Gabs softly and sympathetically.

"Damn straight," added Loz. "Fuck all the other shit and the directors, the council, everything; think about that. None of that metal on your legs, no crutches again, back in the prime of your life. What person wouldn't want that?"

"You still don't understand. Neither of you has thought it all the way through. The sacrifice they're asking me to make is unthinkable. It's the worst thing anyone could ever ask of me, especially...after what I've been through. And watch your language, Loz."

"What is it that we aren't understanding, Mum? I don't see a downside to it. You get to go back in time to a younger, healthier you and get to save the world. Mum, you'd be the saviour of the planet, a hero for all time. They'll be erecting statues of you all over the planet. They..."

"Would do no such thing. If it succeeded then the cataclysm would not happen and none of this," she said waving her arm around to indicate life underground, "will have come to pass. If it doesn't happen no one will know what I did. Whatever happens at my instigation will have no effect on anyone except..."

"Except?" both children asked at once.

Loz and Gabs watched in amazement and concern when they spied a single tear escaping their mother's eye. Neither of them had seen her cry since before the accident. In some weird assumption they both made, they believed her tear ducts had been destroyed in the crash. Rachelle Rizzoli never showed weakness, never released tears and never felt the slightest amount of self-pity, though she possibly had more justification than any other person in UCA.

"You," said Rachelle quietly.

"Huh? What about us?"

"Knowing what you know about me, our lives leading up to this," indicating herself, "do you honestly believe I could go through all that again?"

"Whoa! Of course not. How could you even entertain that thought? No way would we expect that. Why? That doesn't have to be repeated."

"Where do you think you two came from?" she asked sadly.

"Mum?"

"You are the beautiful product of that horrendous union between two people that never should have been together. I should not have allowed it to go as far as it did. But it did and you are the result of that. I can't give that up but I can't repeat the acts that accomplished the miracle. No one can or should ask that of me, no one. It is an unthinkable demand to make of me. One I refuse to consider."

"I still don't understand this, Mum. We're here, alive and well. You go back in time before...him and save the world," said Loz with a puzzled expression.

"I go back to a time before him. When I went for the job

interview. If I don't repeat the acts leading up to your births, then you never enter the world. You cease to exist in this one, this timeline. Either you collapse in a heap and die, or you fade away. I won't do that and I should never have been asked. It's an impossible request to make of a mother."

"Didn't consider that," admitted Loz with surprise.

"Would it happen that way, though? It sounds..."

"Far-fetched? If we accept that this whole idea is born of fact, that they *can* do what they say, then it stands to reason. I'm no expert on time travel or paradoxes. I don't think anyone is. But logic says it's so in my mind. If I don't repeat the past as far as the relationship is concerned, then a millisecond after you were supposed to have been born in that timeline, Gabs, it's curtains. You would no longer exist. Loz follows after that when it was time for him to be born. You cannot exist if you aren't made by the two people that made you. I can't even explore the thought of trying to replicate you with someone else. Your genetic make-up, everything you are, came from a combination of two specific humans, your mother and father. No other combination will produce the two children whom I love and adore more than anything in the world."

Loz and Gabs were stunned by the pronouncement and the overwhelming amount of love and affection coming from a mother who had been so bitter and loveless for so very long. Gabs shared a tear with her mother, while Loz gaped at the pair.

"Don't get me wrong, kids. The pain and suffering I experienced from that doomed union is something I'd be more than prepared to repeat if it meant having you two again. After all, childbirth surpasses all those pain thresholds. But I cannot and will not allow, or live through, the punishments and abuse meted out to my children by that monster. Nor would I abide the humiliation and degradation I experienced again. Like I said before, no man will ever lord it over this woman while I have breath in my body."

Gabs and Loz stared long and hard at one another, communicating silently, reading each other like open books and finally nodding their heads in agreement.

"This goes beyond us, Mum. We can't let you turn this opportunity down for the sake of two children who are insignificant and mean nothing in the long run. This is about saving the world, not just us or even Australia. What you could do would make all this crap go away. Mum, you need to do this," implored Gabs.

"No! I refuse to entertain the idea and I won't be coerced by anyone. It's out of the question. I will not go through that again."

"Then don't. Forget about us. Don't get involved with our father. We can understand what it would mean for you. We went through our own shit with him. We remember having to help you off the kitchen floor all those nights when he came home pissed to the gills, then went to work on us once he was done with you. We would never expect anyone to go through that."

"I said I won't be coerced. I said I wouldn't entertain the idea, and I meant it. I won't hear another word on the subject. Go get ready for bed if you've finished your meal. You each have early starts in the morning. Neither of them moved. GO!" yelled Rachelle.

The young adults, looking like they had the weight of the world on their shoulders, departed the table reluctantly. They each said their goodnights and delivered a peck on their mother's cheek before exiting the small kitchen area. Leaving Rachelle to brood over the conversation and the events of the day once more. Though she remained adamant in her refusal to contemplate the ludicrous proposal, she couldn't help the barrage of thoughts assailing her troubled mind or reliving the conversations with her revered kids.

How noble and mature of them to consider the wider picture. Rachelle's breast swelled with pride at the wisdom exhibited by her youngsters. It would be anathema for her to consider a life without her children. It was a sacrifice that she was unwilling to contemplate. The impossible scenario washed through her mind.

Even if she decided to go ahead, exact timing had everything to do with those vital combinations required to produce identical children to the ones she enjoyed. Re-enacting the precise times and conditions in which her children were conceived would be so impossible that the odds were astronomical, worse than winning a lottery. It was proving difficult to remove thoughts about it from her mind. There was no way she could countenance the proposition.

Going way beyond her stoic resolve and stance on the matter of alcohol after her disastrous brush with the evil fluid, Rachelle decided that she needed the liquid fortification at that point. There was a bottle of bourbon in a hidey-hole that Rachelle was sure the kids had never found. So, it came as a huge surprise when she spied the half-empty bottle. Alcohol had ruined her marriage and ruined her body as a direct result. It was always something she hoped to discourage and prevent in her children when they came of age.

Then she suddenly recalled a night not so long ago, on Gabs' birthday, when she rose from her bed in the middle of the night to get a drink of water and found the kids sitting quietly at the kitchen table. The tableau she came across was odd somehow and the kids had a startled look on their faces, like rabbits in headlights. Too tired, sore and exhausted to pursue her suspicions, she filled her glass with water and returned to her bedroom. Now that she thought about it, she recalled the strange aroma from that night and the odd smiles on her children. They were plastered!

"You sneaky little shits!" she accused softly with a smile.

There was so much fun and enjoyment the kids had missed out on. She recognised her shortcomings in the bitter, twisted person she had become. The anger that ate away at her soul never allowed her to be the kind of mother she wanted to be. The kids deserved better than her if they were reduced to sneaking grog behind her back. Only a day ago Rachelle would have let them have it with both barrels if she'd discovered the half-consumed bottle.

They were adults, with intellects and individuality on a par with their mother, albeit without the degrees. Universities were a thing of the past. Everything they knew was taught by Rachelle and their employer once they were of working age. Many vocations were off the cards with life in UCA. No one learned about meteorology anymore. What would be the point? No weather underground, that's for sure. Entertainment was a thing of the past. No TVs, movies, theatre, concerts, nothing like that. So very much of what made humans unique was lost when the world ended.

The liquor burned its way down Rachelle's throat as she swigged straight from the bottle. The guilt she felt bothered her. It was preached by her long and often as her kids were growing up about the dangers of alcoholism. They'd seen it with their own eyes, experienced the devastating effects of it. It wasn't her right to subject her children to it, wasn't right for her to have alcohol in the cubby-hole they called their home on orange.

Rising from the table with the support of her crutches, she grabbed the bottle angrily, pouring the contents down the sink. The demon fluid would not influence Rachelle Rizzoli. That was something she couldn't abide, a loss of control or the effect it might have, the respect she might lose in the eyes of her children. It was a road she would not travel no matter how much shit was flung at her, no matter how much pressure she had to endure. Life wasn't fair and getting drunk wasn't the answer. Alcohol only added to the problems.

In her younger years, she had partied hard with the rest of her generation, consuming as much, if not more than her fair share of booze. The drinking became part of her adult life after she was married; socially, she liked to believe. The shared habit with her husband became problematic once children came along and Rachelle knew she had to curtail her indulgences to be a fit mother. Her husband felt no such constraints and his consumption seemed to escalate to make up for Rachelle's share.

Feeling a modicum of relief for sticking to her resolve, Rachelle threw the empty bottle into the trash recycling chute. Most of UCA's trash was either recycled or upcycled into new uses like new coatings for all the metal frameworks and gangways to cut down on the noise. The first ten levels had all received the coatings, reducing noise to the barest minimum. Rachelle had to bang her crutches on the walls to make sure she made as much noise as possible if she found herself up there. It was a shame, she thought, that she had to make such an effort to cause all the toffs some discomfort.

After she turned everything off to retire to her room, Rachelle sat on the end of her bunk feeling the first vestiges of depression descending upon her. It was such an imposition on her, such a callous act. As if she didn't have enough guilt thrust upon her by her lousy decisions in the past! They have to heap the future of the planet and all her inhabitants on her shoulders? What a fucking trip! *Could they do it? Could they do what they suggested?* It was a huge leap of faith to accept. It was straight out of one of those bad sci-fi movies they used to make.

After a while of thinking through it all, Rachelle realised there were many questions she should have asked before she acted, before she assaulted the Chief Director and stormed out. The question of exactly how the transfer was accepted by the recipient wasn't clear to her. Well, a great many things weren't clear to her. It was bullshit. It had to be bullshit. Digitising the entire brain? Get real! Shooting that data package through an artificial wormhole produced in a laboratory! *INTO THE PAST!*

"Bull-fucking-shit! Nuh-uh, no freaking way. Gotta stop even thinking about this crap, Rache. You'll only do your head in.

What if? It can't have been an elaborate hoax. Shadforth wouldn't have stooped to such a low just for her benefit. He just wouldn't! All that stuff from the two eminent scientists can't have been fiction, surely? Their names were known to Rachelle who kept up with science as best she could while in UCA. She wasn't privy to any secret experiments, but she did keep abreast of who was who in academia. It was easy information to get if you knew where to look. Her position as a teacher, albeit at the bottom of the rung, gave her some advantages and privileges, like a list of the top minds in their fields for verification or information pertaining to the curriculum.

There was just enough information divulged from the doctors to make it all sound possible. A wave of the hand and hey-presto: flux capacitors and digitised brains. All that was missing was the cool DeLorean. A smile crossed her face at the thought of that ancient movie and its subsequent sequels.

It was difficult to get her head around the paradoxes, or potential paradoxes at play. It was 2145 when Rachelle went for the interview and got the job. Married in late 2145 and already pregnant. Gabrielle was born in 46 with Lorenzo nine months later on the dot. Her life was destroyed in 2150 when Rachelle was involved in the event that made her a cripple and the worst kind of mother and woman possible.

It was while she was in the hospital with her horrific injuries, hovering near death's door for months in the ICU, that she once more came in contact with Dr Thoms, who'd heard about the tragedy to befall his favourite student. He was a perfect gentleman, attentive, supportive and displaying his emotions on his sleeve, unbeknownst to Rachelle. For almost a year, Dr Thoms became her constant bedside companion, as she drifted in and out of consciousness, regaling her with his discoveries and his experiments with a laser drill that would enable him to drill deep enough to tap into the richest thermal pockets available.

He explained unnecessarily how conventional drilling would never achieve the depths involved to gain the riches of energy available many kilometres beneath the surface. During Rachelle's lucid spells, she listened with rapt attention to her mentor and newfound friend, grateful for the distraction from her suffering and discomfort. Not for one moment did Rachelle ever suspect the friendship to be one anything more than one of mutual respect and common interests.

Had she been more attuned to the realities surrounding her while she remained in that state of constant flux, she may well have learned of the man's obvious desires and attraction. One thing above all prevented Rachelle from ascending through the layers of mist in her brain: him. The ultimate cause of her injuries.

True, she may have been responsible for her actions immediately before the event but...he...was the reason she responded as she did. He, her husband, was the cause of all the hardship leading up to that fateful night. Robert Angelo Rizzoli, the bane of her existence and the previous love of her life. It hurt her to say the name, even think it. It hurt down deep, a long way from the physical abuse he meted out regularly.

The damage caused to Rachelle Rizzoli had occurred long before the accident when she finally laid down the law. Like many women, Rachelle never saw it developing. Not clearly, not objectively. Not like an independent woman of the 22nd century with a PhD in geophysics. Not like the tomboy who followed her father around on his prospecting trips through central Queensland, wearing khaki shorts and rugged boots rather than short black dresses and stilettos while attending high school proms like the other airheads in her class.

It should have been obvious to a woman like that. Though she had become besotted by the boy when they met, she was never one to be in the thrall of a man like her classmates. Never one to be subservient in the least. Her mettle was made of sterner stuff than the candy floss of other females desperate to become a Mrs so and so, eager to push out a single child into the messed-up world.

Unfortunately, Rachelle wasn't overly possessed of a good memory when it came to anything but rocks and geographical formations. The contraceptive pill required the taking of said pill every day. Not every other day or even every other week, as it turned out. It was difficult for her to process the information the doctor imparted as she sat behind the desk, having just killed the rabbit. The growing pangs of nausea did have a cause after all, just like her boyfriend suggested.

Robert persuaded her to visit his doctor, the one who had taken care of his family for as long as he could remember. The Italian migrant doctor, who specialised in other Italians living in Australia because he spoke their lingo, nodded his head gravely as he spoke in halting English to the stunned young woman sitting opposite. Though his religion forbade it and it was abhorrent to his oath as a doctor, he knew this woman would probably approach the possibility of getting rid of it. He was prepared for it, though he would never acquiesce to such a thing, nor would he refer her to someone who could.

It came as quite a surprise to the doctor and Rachelle when she simply smiled and clasped her midsection lovingly after she finally regained her composure. Newly hired by the Department of Energy with a glorious future that was all but mapped out, Rachelle discovered that she retained some normal female emotions after all. She wasn't simply a female in male's clothing with the hindrance of female parts! It was a remarkable revelation to her that she found herself excited to enter motherhood with as much enthusiasm as all the airheads and bimbos she knew. Not that she readily socialised with any of them.

Though Robert was not as enthusiastic as Rachelle, he agreed to get married so as not to have a child out of wedlock in keeping with family tradition and religion. The family accepted Rachelle with open flabby arms and moustachioed lips. The wedding reception was a repast made in Italian heaven once the nuptials were observed in the church and the hundred or so guests made their way to the hall hired for the event.

Though her job was based in the ACT (Australian Capital Territory), Rachelle and Robert continued to live in Brisbane where they both grew up. Commuting to work when she was forced to sit behind a desk and not out in the countryside doing what she loved best, did not bother her too much. Geothermal energy was the ultimate goal of the Australian government and most other world bodies. The mining of fossil fuels had long since been either outlawed as a threat to the environment or too scarce to bother with.

Oil fields, coal mines, gas fields, fracking and all other natural fuels had been exhausted and or forbidden. Green energy had been mandated for many decades with privatisation of the grids fast becoming the self-inflicted wound it was forecast to be. Though the world was slipping down the toilet for almost every nation on Earth that hadn't yet perfected alternative green energy sources, Rachelle was unable to remove the smile on her face.

It wasn't until after the birth that the smile faltered slightly. The first big argument that seemed to start over nothing, saw her husband going into such a tirade that Rachelle wondered where the anger had originated. It wasn't like him at all. His rage, aimed directly at her came out of left field without warning and litte provocation as far as Rachelle was concerned. It might have been over a money matter, she couldn't remember.

Struggling with her patchy memory, Rachelle tried to block the passage of thoughts attempting to rattle her. The past was too painful and the future was gearing up to be worse. UCA had only months left according to Shadforth and his cronies. A decision had already been reached by her and she was immovable on it.

SIX

Immovability was not as concrete as the word suggested. Arriving back in orange after her gruelling teaching sessions with children that didn't care to be educated, Rachelle moved into the kitchen to prepare the night's meal. The silence was surprising. The other occupants of the domicile were invariably indulging in either, noisy personal activities, or engaged in perpetual arguments over...everything!

Sleep had not been forthcoming the previous evening and the thought of a blessed nana-nap, while the joint was quiet, tugged at Rachelle. She was glad she had pre-prepared and frozen a meal for her and the kids a couple of nights ago. All the kids had to do was nuke it in the microwave. Gabs was far more capable than that simple act, however, she tended to be lazy. Loz was a lost cause when it came to food preparation and...well, anything related to matters of domesticity.

A scratch in Rachelle's throat made her to peer upwards at the vents supplying their life-preserving air after it filtered out the toxins from topside. Caught in the moment of reflection, Rachelle ran through some of the facts she knew.

1. The requisite minerals required to manufacture new filters were no longer available to UCA residents.

2. Cleaning and replacing the filters was virtually impossible anyway, rendering the first point moot.

3. The air in UCA was degrading. She had seen the readouts herself of the daily samples.

4. UCA had limited time remaining, regardless of the speed with which the air would deteriorate. Three years or three minutes didn't make a huge difference...

No, it could make a difference. In three years, something could be invented, developed or discovered. Another material from which to make the filters could be found to work. Creating new filtration points below ground might then be considered, as access to topside had been prevented due to a deliberate cave-in of the entrance and a subsequent mandate to leave it that way. It was considered by all the top minds that life topside would not be possible for a further two or three generations at least, if ever.

The volcanic ash cloud covering the Earth's surface would bring about a new epoch without life forms roaming across it for the foreseeable future. Top minds debated all the possible outcomes until they were blue in the face without ever reaching a consensus. A new Ice Age, a reversion to conditions before life began with tropical temperatures creating everything anew once the sun shone again. Or else, it was the doomsayers who held the truth; that Mother Earth had breathed her last; that the volcanic activity would prove fatal for her, ending in a galactic cataclysm.

UCA was constructed with future generations in mind, a continuity of the human race, to emerge into the new world once it settled. Now, it seemed that was a fallacy. Running out of air and time, faster than previously predicted and Rachelle was being asked to abandon her children in the short time they had left to become involved in a flight of fancy that had little to no hope of succeeding, even if everything they told her was factual.

It wasn't fair. Rachelle had paid her dues and then some. Resigning herself to her fractured body and a life without joy beneath the ground, Rachelle had adjusted, albeit with bitterness. Her ticket into UCA had been more or less guaranteed by her procurement of geothermal energy once she had corrected the laser drill configuration. A simple intensity equation correction was all it took to perfect the tool.

During her time under the tutelage of Dr Thoms, Rachelle and her classmates had constantly had to correct their mentor on his woeful math. A brilliant man and mind in every other respect, a man dedicated to his vocation, his calling in life. A geophysicist and volcanologist of unparalleled acclaim. When he began his experiments in the Bougainville Trench, it was assumed by many that Australia's energy problems would be a thing of the past.

Dr Thoms had discussed his laser drill in-depth with Rachelle during his hospital visits. In her befuddled state of pain and semi-consciousness, she never twigged to the possibility of him requiring another mind, a mathematical mind to review his formulae for arriving at the requisite configurations. One simple error in his intensity formula destroyed all life on earth when his laser drill breached the planet's core for a sustained period, unleashing a magma missile that triggered the highly volatile chain of active and dormant volcanoes making up the Pacific Ring of Fire.

The almost incalculable pressure at the centre of the earth had forced a plume of magma to shoot through the brief opening caused by the defective laser drill intended to stop drilling well short of the core. The overshooting laser sliced through the crust and the mantle with devastating efficiency, piercing the cauldron of seething, roiling mass providing the planet with its geomagnetic field, deflecting lethal solar rays and cosmic radiations from the surface of the earth.

It was believed that any penetration of the core, were it ever possible, could produce no harm, nor ever be harvested for samples due to the enormous pressure resealing the puncture instantly. A sustained puncture, however, allowing a stream of molten minerals to shoot up the path drilled by the laser, even if only for a fraction of time, found its way into the hotbed of instability around the deep trench, triggering the biggest catastrophe to befall the planet since the extinction-level event that had wiped out the dinosaurs.

Life on the surface was bad enough if a single volcano erupted spectacularly. Just ask the residents of Pompeii. Add a Krakatoa, Mt St Helens and around five hundred more like that to the mix and you have the perfect ingredients for the end of the world. Devastating. Cataclysmic. Lethal. Millions of humans died as a direct result of the eruptions and ensuing earthquakes, tsunamis, violent storms, unprecedented weather conditions across the globe. Millions more died from the toxic fumes circling the globe. All existence choked.

Frantic efforts were made to construct the undercities across the planet to save humanity. The expense didn't matter. Money was a thing of the past, worthless. Everything that once mattered held no meaning in the new conditions. Once news of the lotteries were announced, total anarchy erupted. With gas masks and guns, the gangs formed and began the systematic destruction of life as it was once known. The lottery winners, one hundred thousand Australians, were gathered in a secret compound where they were processed and sent underground as swiftly as possible.

Another thousand top minds in every field of science that mattered made up the remainder of UCA's residents.

UCA was nothing more than an oversized, glorified missile silo. A cylindrical, metal monolith with 10 coloured layers each comprising 10 levels. Every level housed over one thousand residents with enough capacity to expand the total population by a factor of ten. A stricter birth rate was immediately enforced to belay an explosion of new life underground.

The entire edifice was situated around a kilometre beneath the surface. Between each coloured section, was a vast circular, central floor housing gardens and trees, with benches and grass, all under artificial grow lights. It was an absolute necessity, despite the enormous drain on everything from water to electricity, for the residents to have somewhere in each section to congregate and socialise. It was never an attraction for Rachelle, who eschewed public spaces ardently. The stares and derogatory comments she attracted were not worth the effort it required to drag her ugly body across the grassy parks.

The outright vilification and condemnation for Dr Thoms, his momentous blunder and anything at all to do with geothermal energy, carried through to UCA where Rachelle was equally vilified for her part in procuring the energy for the underground city. Even though she was single-handedly responsible for saving everyone's miserable life, she suffered enormously from public rebuke, insults and even the occasional assault by way of expectoration after she was released from custody with only a demotion to show for her crimes.

Dragging her tired body off to her bedroom, the weary woman felt the first vestiges of a serious headache forming in her troubled mind. Unable to shut down the torrent of thoughts assailing her, she was exhausted beyond belief.

Sleep, however, failed her after she'd showered and changed for bed. The effort of releasing her withered limbs from their metallic cages taxed her waning energies, while her mind continued to dwell on the phalanx of images and memories.

It was all so preventable. If Dr Thoms had only...

Sitting bolt upright, Rachelle tried to grasp the elusive light bulb moment. It hovered at the periphery of her conscious thoughts. A catastrophe could be avoided if what? Following through with that line of questioning slowly brought the evasive notion back again.

The idea of going back in time to undo the past seemed ridiculously simple if one thought about it in science-fiction terms where everything was possible. Paradoxes aside, returning to an earlier self, produced a whole set of problems and obstacles. Like, how did one go about changing the faulty device or informing an eminent doctor that his invention was fatally flawed? The answer? One didn't.

The men from upstairs had spoken about sending Rachelle back to the beginning before Dr Thoms' laser drill had become a testable reality. They'd chosen her because of her connections to the man. He was her mentor, after all, and they foolishly believed he'd had a 'thing' for her during her time in university. It would be possible for Rachelle to arrange a meeting with him, a casual conversation over a coffee to catch up and inform him of her good news in being offered a position within the government Department of Energy?

How to broach the subject without alarming him, though? His work on the laser's design was highly classified and his secret at that time. He only revealed the specifics during their shared time in hospital when he felt sorry enough for her to break his code of silence. If Rachelle started talking about it before she knew of its existence officially, he would become immediately suspicious and probably storm off in a huff.

Despite her best intentions to completely dismiss the absurd idea, Rachelle couldn't help but explore possible avenues she could take if any of it was true. Her instinct was to cover herself in glory for discovering the design's shortfall. It was her proudest achievement, after all, despite having been scorned for it.

Something Rachelle said to her children when they were discussing it came to the top of her mind. She'd stated that no one would know of her part if she succeeded in preventing the cataclysm. Gabs spoke of statues in her honour, accolades and recognition. Not true. Not true at all. If nothing happens, then nothing of what Gabs had uttered could happen. The role of an anonymous saviour ran opposite to her sensibilities, though. Pride of achievement in a male-dominated arena held great allure for Rachelle, as much as she was ashamed to admit it.

Viewing past that selfish goal allowed Rachelle to stumble upon a possible solution in the event she went ahead with the insane plan. Anonymity could work in that scenario. No one need know of Rachelle's intervention and Dr Thoms would be granted a gift.

"Idiot! Stop thinking like that Rache. Stop thinking at all. Go to sleep. Fuck.

SEVEN

"Miss? Miss, are you alright? Can I get you a glass of water?" asked the elderly woman with a tight grey bun atop her head and a pair of outlandish spectacles perched on the end of her beak-like nose.

The young woman in front of Alice Beatz swayed suddenly in mid-sentence. It did not bode well for the applicant to react so unfavourably to the line of questions being levelled at her. It should have been expected by the young woman. Alice made sure each applicant for the position was sent all the relative information regarding the interview process. It might be judicious to send the woman down for her medical exam immediately if there was something of concern with her. That would eliminate the need for further questioning if the doctor found a medical condition she had neglected to divulge in her CV.

What the fuck? Where am I?

"Who are you?"

"Why, Alice Beatz. I introduced myself at the beginning. Are you ill?"

"Sorry, no. I'm...fine...I think. My apologies, ma'am."

"I realise these long interviews can be quite stressful for some. Are you sure you don't need a moment and perhaps a drink of water?"

"That might not be too bad an idea. Just a drink of water and I'll be good to go. Do you have a fountain or a vending machine close by?" asked the interviewee.

"I'll fetch you a glass of water from the lunchroom. Wait there a moment, please?"

"Sure."

What the fuck!

"Who is that? Who said that?" the interviewee asked, swivelling around to locate the owner of the voice.

One moment she was sitting in front of the old bat answering about a million questions, the next she went all light-headed. Then she heard a voice, but there was no one around and even the old duck had left.

No, don't tell me...

"Don't tell you what?"

"I didn't ask you to say anything, dear," said Alice returning with a glass of cool water that she placed before the applicant.

Despite the young lady's credentials and impressive resume, it was looking more and more like she would be unsuitable for the position. Alice Beatz was nothing if not proficient in her HR duties when it came to weeding out the undesirable applicants for any government position. Anyone coming under her purview would get the full treatment and be offered no leeway or favour no matter how perfect they appeared on paper. It was her duty, no, her pleasure, to ferret out the problems and inconsistencies or outright lies of applicants who came before her.

"Is there anything you'd like to...confess?" asked Alice with an indignant look.

"Confess?" asked the young woman in confusion.

"The medical examinations are quite thorough, you know? Anything you'd like to reveal now that wasn't listed on your résumé?"

"I don't have any sort of medical condition if that's what you're suggesting," she explained uncertainly.

Bullshit!

The young woman used all her will to keep from saying anything. She remained silent while the old bag looked down her bloody great hooter at her with a look of superiority on her features.

Yep, she was a smug bitch, that's for sure.

"So, no medical condition that would cause you to become light-headed in the middle of an interview?"

"Put it down to some nerves and not enough calories for breakfast? I'm good to go if you want to continue?"

Alice Beatz looked disappointed. She could have sworn she was about to flush one out. If it wasn't for her outstanding CV, Alice would have dismissed her to the next step already; medical. They would have found anything if there was anything to find. The woman appeared to have recovered well after drinking some water. Maybe she had some womanly problems to deal with? Alice was so glad to have passed that particular time of life, though she suffered greatly from hot flushes as a result. It came on suddenly and could see her sweating like a labourer on the coolest day in Brisbane.

"One last question then. I think we've covered all the main criteria. What are your ambitions?"

"Do you mean on a personal or professional level?"

Professional, you idiot!

"Professionally, of course," said Alice with a hint of annoyance.

"Besides hoping to be the one to discover a means to end the energy crisis?"

"Rather grandiose expectations?"

"If I was offered the position, it would be for that purpose, wouldn't it? Isn't that why there is a position available? Or have I got that wrong? I did say *hoping* to be that person, not expecting to be. However, I do think it pays to be positive about one's abilities rather than expecting to fail. Sorry if that's the wrong answer. I am honest to a fault, I'm afraid."

And just as smug as the bitch in front of you too.

"Well, I think that will probably be all from me today. You're scheduled for a lunch break next then you have your full physical and medical examination. I do hope we won't find anything we haven't disclosed?"

"Might open an eye or two but that's probably it," replied the young lady.

"Harrumph! You will find only female clinicians cleared to examine our female applicants."

"Might open more than just two eyes then?"

"Not sure what you could mean."

No, she can't and you need to stop preening.

"Where do the applicants go to get a bite to eat around here?"

"All the food you could ask for is down in the Queen St Mall. Just take the elevators back down to the ground floor but make sure you arrive back here no later than one. Tardiness will not be tolerated," said the prim and proper Alice Beatz.

"Ahh, ladies' room?" asked the applicant.

"To the left of the elevators. Now, if there's nothing else?" she asked impatiently.

"Sorry to take up your valuable time, ma'am."

In the bathroom, the young woman wiped the sweat from her brow then washed her face with cool water.

"What the fuck is wrong with me?" she whispered to her image in the mirror.

I'd like to know the same fucking thing.

"Who...who's there? This isn't funny."

After checking all the stalls to make sure she was alone, the young lady leaned heavily against the sink.

It's no joke. I'm just as pissed off as you.

"Are, are you real?"

I wish I knew. I can't remember what happened exactly. I woke up and here I am.

"Where?"

Where what?

"Where are you?"

Pretty sure I'm in your head.

"Fuck, I'm turning schizophrenic. I'm hearing voices in my head. I need a drink."

That won't solve anything and you're bound to blow the interview if you do. You need this job...badly, and so do I."

"Okay, okay, this is getting totally weird. Who are you and how do you know about my interview?"

Get ready for it. You might want to be sitting for this.

The young lady moved to one of the empty stalls where she lowered the lid before taking a seat.

"Wait, can you...see me?"

Umm, sort of. When you look in a mirror I can.

"How is that possible?"

I'm seeing through your eyes.

"This is so, not happening to me right now. I seriously don't need this shit in my life. I have to concentrate on the interviews today and I can't be hearing voices. If the doctors get a hint of that, I'm done."

You're not going nuts. You can hear me loud and clear, right?

"I'm sure the loonies all say they can hear real voices. Who are you supposed to be, a female God?"

Ha-ha. Not bloody likely. You ready? My name is Rachelle.

"Oh shit, you're telling me I'm nuts. That I'm hearing myself?"

No...and...yes...sort of. Listen, I'm you, Rachelle Rizzoli.

"Who the fuck is Rachelle Rizzoli," the woman voiced in a growing panic.

Sorry, shit. I forgot we aren't married yet. Rachelle Shaw. I'm Rachelle Shaw, or I was.

"Why are you terrorising me today of all days? Who is this and how are you doing it?"

You need to calm yourself down, Rache. You only have till one o'clock to absorb what I'm about to tell you. Then you have to go back and complete the most important interview of your life. You will have to bring your A-game and forget about me until we get it done.

"We? No way am I getting this job with you talking to me. Just tell me who you are first."

I already told you. I'm Rachelle Shaw after I got married and acquired the name Rizzoli. I'm you after a lot of shit happened. I am just having some difficulties adjusting to this myself. My memories are off somehow. I have to concentrate hard just to make a connection or two before the fuzziness comes back.

"How convenient."

I'm not bullshitting you, Rache.

"Stop calling me that. Only..."

Daddy ever called me that. Yeah, I know. Hurt like hell when he went, didn't it? It's the reason you're here today. If we hadn't accompanied him on all those fossicking trips, listening to him describe all the different minerals and semi-precious stones, we wouldn't have studied geophysics and we wouldn't have applied for this job.

"This is getting scary."

Suck it up and put on your big girl pants, Rache. What I'm going to tell you will blow your mind away. If all this is true, then the year is 2145, right?

"Yeah, so?"

Something bad happens a few years from now. Five years to be exact. A cataclysmic event that has worldwide and everlasting repercussions. I barely survived to make it underground with the rest of Australia's survivors. Without going into a shitload of details right now, even if I could remember it all, I've been sent back in time to prevent that bad thing from happening.

"I am so not listening to you right now. This is pure bullshit and I'm leaving..."

SIT DOWN! You can't leave. Suck it up girly. Now, more than ever, you have to get this job.

"Why?"

It gives you the...something. Shit, I can't think of it. I know how fucked up this sounds, Rache but you have to trust that inner instinct, you have to know I'm telling you the truth. This...this wasn't supposed to happen like this. It should have...I don't know...worked instantaneously. Zeta Waves! It's the Zeta Waves. They should have grabbed a hold of and absorbed the package.

"You're off your nut. Or I am. I need to get some lunch."

That'd be great, only you don't have any money.

"Bullshit, I have twenty..."

Melanie took it. When you get home check the footage on the spy-cam. She sneaks into your room while you're in the shower getting ready for the interview and swipes the twenty from your purse. I kicked her out of the flat when I found out.

Rachelle Shaw checked in her bag to ascertain the truth, feeling dumbstruck when she ratified the voice's statement. She had a twenty in her purse when she checked first thing in the morning. For the first time in Rachelle's life, she felt a deep abiding fear almost paralysing her. She had faced everything on her expeditions with her father. Snakes, bird-eating spiders, cockroaches and everything in between. Nothing had freaked her out until now.

She wasn't willing to accept any of it. Not a bar of it. Yet the voice told her there was no money in her bag. The voice knew her flatmate's name and about her father's pet name for her. She had to admit that the voice had a definite similarity to her own intonation as well. That was as far as she was willing to go, though.

Listen, girly, you need to pull yourself together. Tell you what, I won't bug you unless I think you need some help. Otherwise, I'll shut my non-existent mouth. Okay?

"If you are who you say you are, what the fuck happened to you? I don't sound as crabby as that."

You have no idea. It will have to wait, though. You need to get this job. The fate of the human race and the planet depends on it.

"Oh, no pressure, then?"

That's more like it. Shrug it off and get going. Show them what we're made of. Be careful though. If I talk to you or offer you some help, you can't talk back to me. They'll throw you in the rubber room if you do that.

The arduous afternoon wore on for Rachelle as she faced round after round of gruelling inquisitions. Medical was first after lunch, which was the easiest of them all. Psyche evaluation and aptitude tests, followed by IQ tests and more. Other candidates were dropped as the day progressed, leaving only Rachelle at the end of the day. Even Alice bloody Beatz showed a begrudging approval and shook Rachelle's hand to congratulate her. The formal offer would not be made until the following week by way of a letter from the office of the Minister for Energy.

Rachelle staggered from the inner-city office building around five pm. The foot traffic through the mall was in peak afternoon swing. Rachelle managed to scavenge a few dollars from the bottom of her bag, enough for a decent cup of coffee in one of the cheaper coffee houses up at the non-chic end of Edward St, down towards the botanic gardens. Teetering on her heels, Rachelle Shaw felt woozy, as if she'd had too much booze.

Yeah, high heels suck big time. Nothing better than getting around in my Blundstones for the bush.

"I wish you'd get the fuck out of my head, this day has been a living nightmare."

Get something straight, Rache. You're stuck with me and vice versa. It shouldn't be like this and for that I'm...

"Sorry?"

No. I don't say that word. Not to anyone. Something went wrong with the transfer and my memory is very hazy. Parts are coming back to me, though. Grab a coffee and head into the gardens where we can talk properly without someone overhearing you talking to yourself...literally.

"You're starting to freak me out again. Can't you just disappear as you did earlier?"

Grab your coffee and let's go.

Rachelle Shaw grimaced with the pain of a blister forming from the new high-heels. Not that she didn't look smart in her power suit and stylish heels with matching bag, all courtesy of her flatmate, who was in for such a tongue-lashing once she returned. She just wasn't comfortable in anything but her rugged outdoor hiking gear traipsing through the arid landscapes of outback Australia. A spark of sadness assailed her as she thought about her trips with her dad.

I can hear your thoughts, you know?

"Fuck! Really?"

Yeah, unfortunately. There is some seriously boring shit in this head. I never knew that I was only so far removed from those airheads in school or college. University too for that matter. Fuck, I thought I was better than that.

"Shut up, for fuck's sake. Just. Shut. Up. I can't take this crap right now and I don't need the insults."

Touchy.

Rachelle fumed as she neared the coffee shop with the alfresco tables on the footpath under shade umbrellas. The heat and humidity of the day were still at roasting levels and Rachelle's headache, beginning at the back of her eyes, did not bode well for the evening ahead. Some serious drinking might be in store once she got home.

Right, like that'll fix a migraine.

The annoying voice was ignored by Rachelle as she seated herself at a table beneath the shade of an umbrella. Reaching down, she removed her heels with a sigh just as a soft sound and a breeze wafted over her head. Turning her head while massaging her injured heel to peer through the large window, Rachelle noticed a waiter inside the coffee shop suddenly fall, spilling his tray of drinks. Just as she also noticed a neat hole in the glass, a person appeared beside her.

"Excuse me? I think you may have dropped your pen? It must have fallen out of your bag," said the incredibly handsome man with flowing blonde hair.

Fuck, fuck, fuck! Piss him off, now! It fucking can't be. It just can't be... Did it happen that way? Surely not. I don't remember that.

"Thank you. That's very kind. It's a special birthday present from my dad, so I treasure it."

"You're welcome. Have a nice day."

"Wait, what's your name?"

"Robert. Robert Rizzoli. You?"

"Rachelle Shaw. Wait, did you just say Rizzoli?"

"Yes, why? Have we met before? Pretty sure I would have remembered meeting a lady as beautiful as you if I had."

"No...I...just heard the name recently, is all. Thank you again, Robert."

"Tell you what. I'm playing a gig here in the city tonight at Rosie's. And before you say anything, no, I'm not gay. The original club was a gay joint before it relocated. The new owners returned to the old haunt in Edward Street and transformed it into a rock venue. It's pretty cool. I have a couple of passes with me if you'd like to go with a friend?"

"Any other night and I would have jumped at the chance but I've had a gruelling day doing job interviews and I'm busted. Raincheck, perhaps?"

"Sure, here's my card. Give me a call and if I'm playing somewhere, I'll arrange a pass for you."

"Thank you, Robert. That's super..."

Robert had turned and walked off while Rachelle was tongue-tied. He smiled and waved as he crossed Alice Street to wander left, approaching the Brisbane River. Inside the coffee shop, customers were making a commotion and the sounds of panic could be heard. People began pouring out of the front door screaming. A siren could be heard in the distance.

Something's very wrong here, Rache. If I'm not mistaken someone just got shot in that coffee shop. Get moving. Forget the coffee and head over to the gardens so we can talk.

Rachelle immediately did as she was told for perhaps the first time in her life. She was confused, afraid and thoroughly exhausted. Not to mention just a little bit horny after her encounter. He was totally hot as far as Rachelle was concerned and she would probably be taking him up on his generous offer. The hot asphalt burned her bare feet as she crossed Alice Street to enter the botanical gardens carrying her shoes and handbag.

Rushing to the pond, Rachelle dipped her sore feet into the refreshing water while ducks paddled her way for a handout. Sitting on the soft green grass at the edge under the strong sunlight, made her relax as she cast her eyes upwards.

Wow! I never thought I would see that again.

"What?"

The sun, the sky without tonnes and tonnes of ash floating around. I'd forgotten how beautiful it all was despite the problems.

"What happened back there and who's that incredibly hot boy? I recognised the name you mentioned earlier."

Not sure about back there. Just assuming that a hole in the plate glass window with a waiter behind it toppling over suddenly equals a bullet from a very quiet weapon. I can't be certain but your head may have been in the way of it if you hadn't suddenly reached down to take your shoes off to massage your feet.

"Are you saying what I think you're saying?"

Possibly.

"And?"

And?

"The guy?"

Your worst fucking nightmare. Don't even think about...oh!

"What?"

For the longest time, Rachelle heard nothing from within her head, however, a feeling of deep melancholy washed over her. Rachelle wept.

"I don't get it. What is it? Why am I crying for no reason?"

I just had the most awful, gut-wrenching feeling, like I'd lost someone very, very close to me.

"You mean like when dad died?"

Yeah, only worse.

"Nothing could be worse than that. If you really were me then you would know that. So, I know you're full of shit now. Losing dad was the..."

Was the worst thing for me at the time as well, and for years after. Until...

"Until?"

I don't know. I can't remember. Bad, though. That's for certain. Rache, I'm not lying to you. I have fragmented memories so I can't give you a complete picture but I have a general idea of some parts, possibly the worst bits. Five years from now, Dr Thoms begins experiments with a laser drill at the bottom of the Bougainville Trench to secure a ready supply of geothermal energy to satisfy all of Australia's needs for the next millennia.

Only his drill isn't calibrated correctly. It overshoots the mark considerably, piercing the Earth's core long enough for a plume of magma to shoot upwards before the pressure closes the aperture. That plume, at the extreme velocity with which it was ejected from the core, penetrated the volatile tectonic plates in that area causing a chain reaction of the active and dormant volcanoes in the Pacific Ring of Fire. Within a year the planet is sheathed in an increasing shroud of toxic ash from hundreds of volcanoes erupting at once.

Ten years from now, the last of the lottery winners are ensconced within underground cities across the globe. Life as you know it ceases to exist according to our best guesses. Nothing could have survived topside but an Ark of sorts had been set up within the cities for when the time was right to rise again. Frozen embryos of all the known animals, seeds for grains, trees and grasses. Everything that could be preserved for a future above ground was given top priority before we were sealed beneath the surface.

Technological advancements were made while we were down there. Advancements on the mapping of a human brain, advancements in physics where the space-time continuum is concerned and much, much more. I was offered a mission to go back in time, to enter my younger body and avert the cataclysm. I refused. Something happened that I have no memory of and it seems I was sent back despite my resolve.

I was supposed to take over completely once the transfer was made. No one said anything about both of us occupying the same brain. A new brainwave was discovered which they named the Zeta Wave. It was that discovery that led to the possibility of introducing a new set of instructions to a faulty brain, such as one suffering from dementia.

A sophisticated mapping of a person who showed early signs of the condition allowed a binary version of that scan to be accepted by the recipient after the brain had begun deteriorating. The Zeta Wave was the key. It latches onto the identical wavelength aimed at it from outside the brain. It allows the recipient to become imbued with the new Zeta Wave entering its space releasing the information stored within the waves.

Utilising that function, the eggheads then found a way of building a time machine in a lab. Essentially, a time fracture was produced in an artificial vacuum, creating an Einstein-Rosen bridge. It lasted for only microseconds. The data package containing the digitised brain could be shot through the bridge on a photonic beam, through time, into a younger person. I was forty-seven years old when I was told about all this.

"That's quite the tale. Makes for a great book or movie. You can't seriously expect me to swallow any of it, though?"

It doesn't matter what you think.

"What's that supposed to mean? And stop being rude. Man, you are so nasty!"

If I understand it correctly, and the first signs of it are there when you felt that wave of depression hit you, you won't be around for much longer.

"Yeah, I get it. Only another five years and doomsday. Jeez! You're as bad as some nutter standing on a street corner with a sign reading, 'The End Is Near'."

No, dumb-arse! You're not hearing me. The new Zeta Wave containing the digitised brain - me - will soon take over completely. It was supposed to happen instantaneously according to the boffins. I have only an inkling as to what happened. A tickle in the back of my memories. Something failed or didn't go according to plan. Shit, I refused the mission, yet here I am. You felt that sadness I was feeling. I can only assume that will get stronger as I start to take over. You will cease to exist in this body when that happens. You will be...redundant in that scenario.

"Fuck you! This is just pure horse shit. Tell me who the hottie is?"

He was my husband. The worst thing that ever happened in my life. He turned into a raving lunatic after we were married, a tyrannical, demented, abusive, chauvinist pig. He made my life a living hell and I have no intention of allowing you to hook up with him. You think I'm in your headspace now? Just you try and call that monster. I'd absolutely forgotten that we met there at that coffee shop. I only recalled the gig I went to when we hooked up afterwards. It was all sweetness and kindness then.

"Hot?"

I choose not to think of any positives from that horrible union. There probably were some, but I refuse to let them colour the truth of what he became. I'm starting to feel your legs through you. You have no idea how good that is. Treasure them pins babe, because they got messed up bad after the shit hit the fan.

"What shit?"

You aren't listening. HIM. He's the shit that hit the fan and caused me more heartache than any woman deserves. He turns into pure evil. The worst of the worst.

"Couldn't have been that bad. What, he slugged you once?"

Oh, you dumb bitch. I can't have been that stupid back then, surely? I'm trying to save you from the worst abuse a woman can suffer besides the physical pain. The mental anguish and agony that man inflicted on me, the brutal subjugation and humiliation I was forced to endure shattered my existence. Broke me at the core of my being. Broke my body in the end and I was never without pain again after that. I am so looking forward to feeling two fine legs beneath me once more.

"No need to insult me. I get it already. What happens now, in your world of impossible make-believe?"

Until I take over your functions, we're limited. I have to draw a detailed schematic of Dr Thoms' laser drill on a computer with some serious technical drawing capabilities. That leaves out your clunker from the 40s.

"Hey, I just bought that laptop. Cost me half my savings."

No kidding. Tell me something I don't know. Like I said, a clunker from the 40s. I'll have to think about this for a bit. It's integral to my plan.

"What plan?"

Fuck me! Will you stop thinking with that hairy twat between your legs for a moment and listen to what I'm saying? Don't you get it? Five years from now the end of the world begins. What they call the doomsday device unleashes unholy hell on this planet and its inhabitants. We're talking total extinction of all life on Earth.

"Thought you said you and the other survivors went underground? Wouldn't be survivors if they didn't, you know, survive?" said Rachelle Shaw in the cattiest tone she could achieve.

Until 2165, yeah. Then the air purifiers crap out and it all comes to a head again. The end, kaput, fini. Are you being deliberately obtuse or just plain dense? Use those grey cells, girl and get with the program. We don't have much time to save it all. Five years may seem a long time but it isn't. And for my plan to work, it has to be implemented in the next year or less. I have to have the corrected details of the laser drill on paper...or disc.

When Rachelle rolled over onto her stomach to get some warm sunshine on her back, a sudden flurry of movement from the water caught her attention. When she continued her roll to the left to sit on her backside again, she became confused by the sight of a duck squawking loudly and splashing frenetically in the shallow water. Rachelle spied a blot of red spreading over the white feathers before the duck simply toppled over onto its side. dead!

RUN!

Rachelle didn't need to be told twice that something terrible and dangerous was happening. Bolting for the nearest clump of bushes, Rachelle swore when she caught her barefoot on an exposed root, tipping her. She stumbled and fell barely a millisecond before the bark flew away from the trunk of the bush next to her.

Stay down. I should have figured it out before. The bullet that entered that coffee shop window to take out the waiter had to have come from the direction of the gardens and was definitely aimed at you. I thought it may just have been a case of being in the wrong place at the wrong time in the semi-lawless environment of the 40s. Someone wants you dead, and I can't let that happen or I go with you and I have no way of going back to where I came from.

"Why would someone be trying to kill ME? Are you out of your mind?"

Yes, I am, dearie. Hmm. You have a point, though. I wasn't a wanted woman back then and none of this rings any bells, so...

"So?"

History is changing already. It isn't you that they're after. It's me. That can only mean someone from my timeline came back as well, with instructions to stop me. He said they had already sent people back but they didn't have the connections to make a difference.

"You may be in my head but you're mumbling and I can't hear what you're saying. Can I..."

Stay down! Use our eyes, scan the area, find where the sniper is hiding.

"S-sniper?"

Would you prefer the word assassin?

"This cannot be happening. None of this is real. I'm going to wake up in my bed real soon and have to prepare myself for my interview. That's it! I was having a stressful night with these horrible nightmares over the upcoming interview. My alarm will go off and I'll be back in bed."

Crawl, you idiot! Crawl your way along this row of bushes until we get to the river path. The small retaining wall beside the path will offer you shelter until you get to the gate, then make a run for it back towards the city.

"I'll just wait here until I wake up. You need to realise that you're just part of a bad dream."

You need to realise that unless you move, you'll be dead.

Someone wants me dead and I'm in your body whether you like it or not... Hey, what do you know, I'm feeling them. Now I just need to worm your way along here if I can...

Without the use of her arms, Dr Rizzoli pushed the body of her younger self along the ground like a drunken caterpillar. Leaves and bark mulch were being shoved up Rachelle Shaw's nostrils and into her mouth if she opened it to say anything.

"Phtooey, ouch! Stop. Can't breathe with this shit getting up... Argh! My legs! I can't feel my legs."

No shit, Sherlock? Use your fucking arms and help move us out of here.

"Ooh, Melanie is so going to kill me when I hand back her business suit. I think it's torn."

Fuck, Rache, just move it, will you? How would Melanie feel getting it back full of bullet holes once she claims it from the morgue after it's removed from your dead body? You can't feel your legs because I have control of them now. It's part of the process, see? Pretty soon you'll be the voice in my head and I'll have complete control of my young, healthy body. Which is staying that way, you hear? No more midnight snacks or drinking. No more bloody chocolates. Move now, move. Crawl, you lazy, fat-arse bitch.

"This is...so unfair," said Rachelle Shaw using her arms eventually to assist in the crawling.

Boo-fucking-hoo. Keep going.

EIGHT

Melanie was furious about the condition of the business suit. She wasn't quite so vociferous when she was shown the footage of her thievery by Rachelle Shaw. Given her marching orders to vacate the premises, a small flat in Spring Hill leased under Rachelle's name alone, Melanie grew quieter still. It was well-known how difficult it was to find affordable accommodation close to the city. Rachelle would have to find another flatmate soon to ensure she could continue to pay the rent. Until she started getting paid by her new employer. Then, she would be on easy street for the foreseeable future.

Christ, this place is a dump! Don't either of you lazy shits ever bother to clean?

"I left home just because of that sort of shit. I don't need another mother, thank you," said Rachelle wearily.

A sudden silence inside her head made Rachelle wonder if she had gone too far. The voice did save her bacon, after all. Rachelle would have had no idea that she was an assassin's target. If the voice hadn't warned her she'd be dead meat on the slab at the morgue, with her mother having to identify the corpse.

"Sorry. Didn't mean to be a bitch about it. Hello, you there?"

S-something just jolted a memory. It's there, right there but I can't seem to grab a hold of it. Oh well, it'll come of its own accord. Pack your things.

"What? Why would I pack my things? I live here."

Exactly. The assassin will know that and come looking for you.

"Look, how could you possibly know all this?"

It's a process of logical elimination. I'm you and I have memories of this time in my life. In 2145 no one was trying to kill me. Pretty sure I would have remembered that. Funny though, because somewhere in the back of my mind that memory of the day I went for the interview is getting weaker...changing... Shit!

"Fuck, now what?"

It will be changing, you see?

"No, I don't see at all. What are you on about?"

History, my history is changing because of the events today. That stuff never happened in my time. I just went home after the coffee and had a row with Melanie after I viewed the footage. The new experiences we went through today, where they differ so much from the ones I experienced back then...now, will slowly filter through to me. So, my new history will eke its way through to me over the continuum. If that's true, then whatever it is I'm missing may be lost forever if I fuck with my history too much. I can't let that happen for some reason. It's way too important, I feel that.

"I cannot handle this. You're talking way over my head."

Crapola! You're a scientist and a sci-fi buff. Remember how often you watched that ancient movie with the DeLorean in it and that other one with the time machine? You know what an Einstein-Rosen bridge is. We learned about that in our physics classes. Essentially, just a matter of folding the space-time continuum to connect two disparate points in space and time. That could be billions of light-years apart and thousands of years, or it could be just a few metres and a few seconds apart.

"Theoretically," Rachelle said with a sneer. "And can you please stop pacing around on my legs!"

You have no idea how good it feels to be whole again...from the waist down, anyway.

"At least walk me over to the kitchen so I can make us...me...a cup of coffee. I didn't even get to order one earlier. Remember?"

We don't have time, Rache. Someone is after me and willing to shoot me. I don't know whether that's because I know something I shouldn't, I pissed someone off or it's to prevent me from succeeding in my mission. Either way, we're in deep shit if we don't get out of here. They'll know where I live in this timeline. Even if they don't, it won't take them long to find out.

"Jeez, why couldn't they just shoot your brain into Dr Thoms and get it over with?"

It doesn't work that way. The discovery of the Zeta Brainwave that made the transfer possible can only work on the original host because the Zeta Wave is as unique to each individual as fingerprints. The wave pulses at extremely low frequencies and oscillates in an infinite range of cycles. It is the Zeta Waves of the recipient that react to the identical incoming waves, latch onto them and incorporate those into the host with the...

"Something wrong? With the, what?"

The digitised brain scan is embedded in the wave. I think I just figured something out. If a brain scan records and digitises a human brain, then that data package is reduced to a bunch of zeros and ones...binary! That means that there is probably software around in 2165 that can open those files, read them and...

"Christ this is annoying. And?"

Manipulate them. Change them. Delete things. That's why there are gaps in my memory. Only they haven't managed to fully interpret the information regarding emotions around those memories. They removed certain parts of my history for some reason but either forgot about or couldn't access the emotional consequences of those events, embedded in the code. I felt an overwhelming sadness at one point, which you felt as well. It's related to a memory I no longer possess. The bastards fucked with my brain!

"Who?"

I don't know that either. I remember talking to a couple of scientists about all this but I don't think they were pulling the strings. Someone else was behind it and I have no recollection of who.

"Sucks to be you," said Rachelle Shaw flippantly, imitating some character from an old sci-fi movie, one which she couldn't place. Something to do with a robot, she thought.

And you think I'm annoying? When did you start being an airhead like those bimbos we hated in school?

"When did you lose all zest for life to become a twisted, ugly soul?"

The day I became a broken human.

The flat comment made Rachelle Shaw pause. It was information given to her before, only not in such a grim manner. The voice had mentioned the use of her legs and other things all pointing to an abusive relationship that ended in tragedy somehow. If anything the voice said was true, the tragedy stemmed from that boy she met at the coffee shop, the hottie.

The serious nature of the consequences, if true, would be worth avoiding. Rachelle made a mental note to lose the business card handed to her. A new career awaited her in a week or so and the voice was making all sorts of demands on her. She didn't have the use of her legs anymore and felt a similar tingle extending along her left arm that foretold the possible loss of that limb to the voice as well. All that did not bode well for a burgeoning relationship, anyway, so, no biggie.

Rachelle Shaw was a scientist with a serious penchant for sci-fi., she admitted. While her practical self eschewed the whole premise put forward by the voice, her inner appetite for science fiction had been tantalised. It would be one helluva trip and possibly everyone's dream to place an older head into their younger body. Live life over with a shitload more experience and intelligence the second time around? In the prime of someone's life? Fucking unbelievable and totally awesome!

The worry about it, though, came in the form of the gaps in the voice's memory, the idea that someone was out to murder her, and the fact that she wouldn't be an active part of it once the old bitch took over completely. That would be a real bummer! Part of the reason Rachelle wasn't willing to pay too much attention to the voice when it rattled on about that, was that Rachelle was desperately trying to figure out a way of avoiding that particular scenario. Disappearing did not sit well with her. It was her life up to then and she didn't want someone else, even her older self, taking over.

The alternatives, if there were any, caused just as many alarm bells to sound. Getting rid of the voice somehow meant she would be unprepared for the eventualities to come, the pitfalls to avoid and, most onerously, the end of the world. Keeping the voice forever as a little Jiminy Cricket in her head would similarly be a catastrophe in the making. It would drive her completely batty eventually. They would have to put her in a rubber room and throw away the key once she started arguing with herself. Probably try and kill herself if it got bad enough.

You do realise that I can hear all that?

"Shit, really?"

Duh! I'm in your brain!

"You mean I don't have to talk out loud to you?"

Yes! I'm. In. Your. Buh-rain!

"Why didn't you tell me sooner instead of letting me look a complete idiot?"

I did, and you don't need any help from me in that department right now. It's going to be a moot point real soon if you don't cooperate with me to move those arms and start packing some shit you need.

"Alright, alright. Sheesh! Where are we going?"

Somewhere no one will know about. You'll have to pay cash for a motel room for a while.

"Get real. I can hardly afford the rent and some baked beans till next payday."

Hmm. In that case, you'll have to sell, you know what?

"I don't know what."

Yeah, you do.

A sharp intake of breath indicated that Rachelle Shaw did know what...and didn't like it.

"No," she said in a hushed tone.

Why are you whispering?

"In case someone overhears."

I'm. In. Your. Head! You don't need to talk at all!

"I get it, I get it, already."

No, you don't, otherwise, you wouldn't still be talking out loud. Doesn't matter anyway, there isn't anybody here.

"You can't mean what I think you mean."

Yeah, that's exactly what I mean. Daddy's nugget. Take it to a pawn shop or a gold dealer. Worth a small fortune at the gold prices of the day.

"I can't do it. I won't do it. It's from..."

I know who it's from, Rache. I just told you. I remember the day we went out and found that one. Daddy searched all over the bush with the metal detector and found squat. I get up and have a go while he takes a break for coffee and I find the mother of all nuggets compared to the other stuff dad found. Can't believe Dad let me keep it. He always said that whatever we found on our trips would always be shared equally, no matter who found it. I saw how disappointed he was when I showed it to him with a big, shit-eating grin on my gob, rubbing it in and trying my best to shame the poor bastard. He just smiled that beautiful smile of his, the one he reserved for me alone and said I should keep it for a very special occasion.

"I never told another living soul about that. Not even, Mum. You could only know that if you've been telling the truth and you are...me?"

Hey there, Rache. Welcome to the real world.

"Shit, um, um, um…'The Matrix'?"

Yeah. One of my favourites from way back.

"I can't quite feel relaxed about any of this. What, what should I call you?"

Be a bit stupid if we call each other the same name, so, call me Rizzo.

"What movie is that from?"

I think there was a musical with that name in it, but I'm using it as a derivation of my last name, Rizzoli.

"You never dropped the married name?"

Sounds weird, doesn't it? You'd think I would have thrown that away as soon I was divorced. I have a feeling I didn't do that for a reason but I can't think what that might be. Could have something to do with that missing information again. So, the nugget?

"Suppose."

Using it to help save your life would qualify as a special occasion, wouldn't it?

"It's just…"

I know. Hard. You've had it with you all those years. It's almost like a best friend.

"It's a bit disconcerting talking to someone who knows everything about you. I can't even think secret thoughts."

Time to go, kid.

NINE

Once they were cashed-up and settled in a small motel on the Gympie highway just past the General Hospital, Rizzo was trying to convince Rache to purchase the latest model laptop. In the end, after Rache refused, it was decided that the library might be a better choice.

They returned to the city on a train. Rizzo worried that the assassin may have hung around the city in the hopes of spotting Rache once it was discovered she'd vacated her residence. The Friday afternoon crowd had vacated the city. The night crowd had not yet filtered in from the suburbs to sample the nightlife on offer. The library in Brisbane Square opened until late on Friday nights.

Rache had showered and changed into comfortable jeans, a pullover and running shoes. Her auburn hair was tied back into a ponytail. Rache was known in the library from her student days, having visited the impressive building regularly. The library computers had all been updated recently but only one had the type of technical drawing software that Rizzo said she needed. The desk housing the computer was at the end of the line with privacy screens on either side of it.

Okay, get us in using your library card.

"You stalking me?" came the all-too-familiar voice to Rizzo.

Shit! Look, you have to say what I tell you, okay?

Rache turned around to face Robert Rizzoli.

"What's the matter, you lost? The pub's down the road," she said with a sneer.

Robert straightened his neck at the odd statement coming from someone who didn't know him from Adam.

"Library's not exactly your style, is it?" Rache asked, following Rizzo's prompts.

"Wow, way to judge someone without a shred of knowledge. I'll have you know I come here every day, pretty much."

"Learning better ways to bend the elbow?"

"Not sure what's gotten into you. I was very mistaken about you and I apologise if you thought I was being forward this afternoon. I don't drink and I never have. I'm here to study for my entrance exams into the Academy of Music."

"They let hard-rock types into the A.A.M. now, do they?"

"You've never heard me play?"

"Looked you up online. Found a couple of clips."

"Oh? Well, that's just to pay the bills and help me to save up for the fees."

"Close to signing a record deal with Vir-Mush, aren't you?"

"How the heck could you know about that? Only spoke to them a couple of days ago. And how could you know about that merger of the two record labels when they haven't announced it yet? You an industry spy, or something?"

"Alright, I'll bite. What are you hoping to study?"

"Classic, of course."

"Classic? What, classic guitar?"

"Piano. The only thing I've ever wanted to do in my life is to play solo, classic piano."

Bullshit! He's a metalhead through and through. A very talented one, I admit, but no way is he or was he ever into classic music and I've never seen him play the piano.

"So, how does one study classic piano in a library?"

"Music theory and scores. They have a fairly impressive catalogue here. One of the best in Australia."

"Sorry about that. I have a very cynical mind these days and it makes my mouth come out with all sorts of shit," said Rache, ignoring the advice of the voice. "I'd love to hear you play one day."

"You still want to come to a gig?" asked Robert, relaxing a little.

"Well, yeah, that too. What I'd like to hear is you playing the piano. Are you honestly good enough to get into the Adelaide Academy of Music? I hear it's almost impossible to get in. They take applications four years in advance from all over the world."

"Yep. My audition and entrance exams come up early next year. I was chosen to audition out of an initial list of three thousand applicants and a shortlist of one hundred. Only four places will be offered for piano. Competition is fierce and applicants have been known to sabotage others."

"How could that happen?"

"You mean apart from crushing the opposition's hands? They

get on the web and leak false information, invent criminal histories, trick applicants into illegal activities then blackmail them. All sorts of shenanigans. Anyway, you have my card. Give me a call sometime if you're interested and we can get together for a small recital. As I said, I'm here to study, so I can't hang around. See ya."

"You cannot seriously expect me to believe he's the Devil incarnate?"

I said evil incarnate.

"Same thing. He's an absolute hottie, well-mannered and trained in classical music with a chance to audition for entry into the AAM. He doesn't look like he could slap his way out of a wet paper bag."

I admit that some of this is unknown to me. It's weird. I caught up with him at one of his rock gigs. I was instantly smitten. A total groupie. I followed his gigs around Brissy for a while and then I buckled down and concentrated on my new job. We dated on and off. We got married in 46 and...

"Don't start that shit again. And?"

Big gap in the memory there. Wasn't long after that he started doing alcohol, then drugs and alcohol. We argued almost all the time. Couldn't agree on anything. We were swimming in money, though. He made a mint from his records and I was earning good coin in the job.

He slapped me the first time a year after we were married. It got progressively worse from then. I ended up in hospital a few times with broken ribs, cut lips and bruising. Then came the cricket bat, his weapon of choice. I nearly died from one of those sessions.

"Why would you stay with someone who did that to you? Is that like that battered wife syndrome you hear about?"

Could be. I'm a bit hazy about why I would persist in that sort of situation. It isn't like me, that's for sure. I can only assume there were extenuating circumstances.

"What a cop-out. So, you were busted up by him and that's how you ended up a cripple?"

No. Not sure of the exact reason or how I worked myself up to it, but I told him one night that I was leaving him. We were in his brand-new Tesla Sportz coming home from an after-show party he more or less insisted I attend with him. He was flying pretty high on a mixture of shit. I'd had a couple of stiff drinks myself, as a way of fortifying myself for the ordeal to come.

At first, there was utter silence. The car didn't make a sound because it was electric. You could hear a pin drop in the car after I told him in a clear calm voice that I'd had enough of being used for batting practice. Then he turned and gave me a malevolent smile that made my skin crawl. He didn't say a word. He just leered at me while flattening the accelerator to the floor.

We were flying down this street and he wouldn't take his eyes off me. How the car kept going straight is beyond me. It went so fast so quickly I could scarcely believe it. That's electric cars for you. Zero to 200 km/h in the blink of an eye...straight for a rock wall past the T section at the end of the road.

Knowing he wouldn't hurt himself or his precious good looks, I called his bluff and told him to do his worst. The ultimate game of chicken with an opponent that couldn't get out of the way. It had to be him that turned in time but he kept his eyes glued on me the whole time.

I could see the wall getting closer and closer out of the corner of my eye. That horrible smile never left his face. The car seemed to go faster if that was possible. Lights at the T section were turning red in the distance with cars starting to cross over from the right and left. The car began a high-pitched whine as it reached its maximum revs.

"Rizzo? What? He stopped or turned, right?"

The last thing I ever heard him say was, 'Meet you in hell, bitch!' The car smashed into the wall at its highest possible speed. The airbags deployed, of course, and all the other safety features of the car helped me to survive the crash until the ambulance got there. They had to use the Jaws of Life to free me from the wreckage. I was barely alive.

I did flat-line half a dozen times over the following months while I drifted in and out of comas. There was hardly a bone in my body that hadn't been broken. I lost half a lung, one of my kidneys and my left eye. I had a permanent droop to my face on the left side and my legs and hips had to be braced externally for years while the bones knitted back in a ghastly parody of the woman I once was. I was a wreck both inside and out. I didn't want to live. I hated everyone and everything. I tried to overdose on prescription drugs at least three or four times after saving them up. I can't remember just how many times it was.

I finally quit eating and drinking altogether. I was in a deep depression and I wouldn't respond to anyone. I just wanted to die. The pain was unbearable, the sight of me was intolerable. I was hideous. A gargoyle without the wings to replace my useless legs. They fed me intravenously, of course, but it didn't matter. I continued to waste away, not wanting to have any more to do with life. I'd given up.

"Oh God, I'm so sorry. That must have been pure hell. You didn't give up, though because you said you went underground sometime after that. What year was it that the thing happened?"

2150 was the year Dr Thoms let loose with the defective laser drill, the so-called doomsday device. Ironic isn't it, that the man responsible for the destruction of the world was the man who brought me back from the brink? He'd heard about my...accident. He came to the hospital every day after he found me. At first, I had no idea about anything. I was comatose most of the time and drugged the rest. He watched my decline with his big sad eyes when he couldn't find the words to help me.

When I became aware enough to resister his presence beside my bed most days, I waved him away with my one good arm. I couldn't talk at that time, you see. My jaw was wired up as well with half my teeth missing or broken. I can't tell you how many times I cut my tongue badly with those broken shards protruding from my gums.

Dr Thoms stayed. I couldn't shut him up. He talked till I was blue in the face trying to make him stop. He prattled on and on about everything including his top-secret laser drill. He told me everything about it, every detail from the hardware to the software and the coding for it. Even then something registered in the back of my mind, some details seemed off and in my dazed state, I wasn't able to identify it.

That mad, magnificent, kind man would not stay away and he finally eked his way through my defences. A year later I was broken, bent and disfigured but I was alive and wanted to stay that way, albeit as a crabby bitch from that moment on.

"Yeah, you haven't lost that particular trait. What about...?"

Because his head was turned to me, when the driver's airbag exploded, his neck snapped instantly. A short and sweet death while he managed to inflict his final act of extended abuse on me. I lived to suffer and that prick got to die without feeling any of it. I learned to hate in that hospital. I learned to be strong, never to bow to the needs of another person for as long as I had breath in my remaining lung. Certainly, no man was ever going to get near me again or attempt to bully me without dire consequences. They said that Dr Thoms had a thing for me and it may have been true given the amount of time he devoted to me in that hospital. But I was dead to any such advances, dead to men, dead to intimacy.

"So, what was it then?"

Hmm? What was what?

"You said it was Dr Thoms that succeeded in reaching you but there was no way that he could be intimate with you. He gave up at some point when that became clear. So, what kept you going after that?"

Overwhelming sadness engulfed them. Rache felt it more the second time around, causing her eyes to well with tears. The voice had retreated for the time being, no longer a hovering presence in her head. The undeniable melancholia that swept over her threatened to undo her as she sat before the blank computer screen, not having so much as hit a key to remove the screensaver.

"Rizzo? Are you there," she whispered. "What happened? Why do I feel so horrible all of a sudden?"

It has something to do with that missing memory. The bastards tampered with the coding once they had a hard copy of my brain. I feel an enormous chasm where there should be something else. It's like having a hold of something weighty in your arms for a long time and when it's placed down, you feel the release of that weight for a time afterwards. Or it could be that we are managing to change history already concerning my timeline and I am experiencing the repercussions of those changes. I think I'm susceptible to anything that happens from now on, that didn't happen in my original past. It's the butterfly effect, where everything you touch, say or do has repercussions down the line for all the persons connected to that.

"I don't get you."

Let's say that I saved someone in my past, say tomorrow. If you don't do that tomorrow, then that person is dead, and everyone related to that person is affected, maybe preventing one of those persons from doing something significant themselves. It's a domino

77

effect that keeps cascading through the decades until it reaches my timeline where it affects me in the here and now.

"Like going back in time to kill Hitler in his crib as a baby? If that happened then we wouldn't have a Second World War and so on?"

Therein also lies a paradox. Theoretically, history cannot be changed. Parts of it may alter certain outcomes such as you mentioned. It wouldn't be Hitler that causes the Second World War. However, it may be that someone else will rise as an evil dictator due to the lack of suppression caused by Hitler's regime. For every Yin, there's a Yang, they say. No, that denotes opposites. No, I mean it only takes the right set of conditions to arise from those altered circumstances in which a new evil persona is allowed to ferment his toxic rhetoric with which to attract followers.

"So, if it wasn't Hitler it would have been another person, making a World War II inevitable?"

Not necessarily, and not at the time when Hitler rose to power.

"That subscribes to destiny or theological origins."

No, it subscribes to a series of events that have already happened. It's like the pages of that book can be minimally altered but not torn out. Whatever happened will have to happen in some way and at some time.

"So, you have no way of preventing the catastrophe that ruined the globe? What's the point then?"

The boffins believed it could be done. I didn't...don't. It's a paradox. A juxtaposition of colliding events within the space-time continuum. If you fuck with that in any way, I'm betting the same or worse will happen at a later date.

"Why bother then?"

Ah, well. That's the question, isn't it? Why am I here? I refused to take the mission, believing that the past was practically unalterable in any significant sense. I know one absolute about myself from my timeline; I am immovable about any decision I've made. I conclude from that troubling observation that I was coerced, forced into 'volunteering'. It may be that I was blackmailed into it. That missing piece of the puzzle may have been the tool they used to get me to agree to the insane scheme. Or, I had no say in it whatsoever.

"How would that be possible?"

If I was rendered unconscious, they could map out my brain, take their time to tamper with the files and send me back here. If that was the case, then my unconscious state may account for the reason the takeover wasn't instantaneous, as I'd been led to believe it would be.

"You mean the length of time it's taking for you to gain control of my brain functions?" asked Rache with an edge of sadness.

*Yes, it shouldn't have happened this way at all. I should have been implanted in your mind and taken over immediately. I know this is cruel for you and hard to accept. Sooner, rather than later, you'll be nothing more than a voice in **my** head.*

"Then I'm gone forever?"

No. You live vicariously through me. Heck, you are me! We'll be combined, is what I meant to say.

"What are we doing here if you say you can't make a difference?"

I'm hoping to mitigate the cataclysm to a smaller less catastrophic event. It's only slim hope, nothing more. My science brain tells me that the past cannot be altered to eradicate a problem altogether. However, I'm here and I may as well try.

"You say you solved the problem with the doomsday device in your time?"

Years after the fact. When I came across the schematics and the coding given to me to decipher after it was found in a flotation safe, I discovered the defect in the density equation used by him to determine the intensity setting of the laser drill. That being:

Mass: 5.972×10^{25} kg

Volume: 5.9722×10^{24} kg

Density = Mass / Volume

= 5.972×10^{25} kg/5.9722×10^{24} kg

= $5,515.3$ kg/m^3

Therefore, the density of the earth is $5,515.3$ kg/m^3

Once the density is established then the laser can be properly calibrated for intensity and restriction parameters.

"That density equation is taught in our first year. Which part of it did he get wrong?"

That's right. His head for math sucked big time while every other part functioned on a genius level. It didn't matter which part he got wrong. He was a brilliant man and a great mentor. Just one stupid error, an incorrect digit in the equation and the intensity settings on the laser were input inaccurately, meaning the laser drill overshot its mark.

"Shouldn't have triggered a global event even if the laser drill penetrated the core. It would have sealed itself instantly once the drill was turned off."

Had it occurred anywhere but on top of the most volatile region on Earth with highly unstable tectonic plates, it probably would have been nothing but a minor eruption well below the earth's crust. The fact that he conducted his experiments so close to the ring of fire ensured a major calamity in the making. It took but a mere second for the magma plume exploding up the shaft to reach several magma pockets connected to the hundreds of volcanoes along the ring. That set off a chain reaction that couldn't be halted.

"What's the plan?"

Simple really. Give him the right information.

"What? Who?"

Dr Thoms. Give him the schematics and the corrected coding.

"If he's already working on the device, why give him the schematics for it?"

Legitimacy. If he sees a simple equation he believes he knows and is told he somehow managed to get it wrong, he'll most likely dismiss it as a hoax or even a joke. If he receives an email detailing the specifics of his device along with all the correct coding, he should sit up and take notice. Nobody knows about the device but him. He told me that while I was in the hospital. It's the one thing that would make him pay attention; fucking with his baby.

"You said the schematics and coding you were given access to were from a flotation safe. I assume that meant Dr Thoms died?"

He was conducting his experiments from a sub-oceanic drilling platform at the base of the Bougainville Trench. One of the first casualties of the cataclysm. Another distinctive first for the esteemed Dr Thoms, as well as being cast as the villainous perpetrator of Armageddon. He was vilified and verbally castrated in the press before everything died. His device and his theories were outlawed under threat of the death penalty for any transgressors.

"Yet, you managed to do it? You corrected the design and used it to capture thermal energy from a deep source on mainland Australia?"

Yeah. Stupid me.

"They didn't give you the death penalty?"

They didn't know what to do with me. Had I model looks and a bubbly personality I probably would have been made a hero, or something. As it was, I was ostracised and made a scapegoat even though I saved the population of Australia and perhaps the world.

"Until you didn't?"

Rub it in, why don't you? Corroding air filters was nothing to do with me. I can't be expected to hold all the answers to everything. I reckon what I did manage was pretty awesome stuff even though it made me a pariah. I think I would have preferred execution to the career they handed me; teacher! I hate teaching and I hate chil...

"What was that?"

I was going to say something that wasn't true and yet, is true.

"Huh?"

I couldn't bring myself to say that I hated children. But I did. I loathed them in the classroom. Sweaty, smelly, horrible, smug little creatures. Sniggering at me behind my back and under their breath. As soon as they're challenged the cowards sink back into the woodwork. Bad as that is, I couldn't bring myself to label all children with the same brand. I guess there must have been one or more that absolved the rest from being besmirched by my generalisation.

"Doctor Rizzoli?" asked the woman suddenly appearing beside Rache.

Don't answer her. Make up something to get her away from you so that we can escape.

"You must be mistaken. That isn't my name," said Rache with a growing sense of dread.

"Oh, right. You aren't married yet. I forgot. You are Rachelle, though, right? I can't remember your maiden name. I'm sure I saw it somewhere in the brief, but I can't put a finger on it."

"Good guess. Yes, my first name is Rachelle. What of it and who are you?"

The tall woman of anywhere between twenty and thirty with strong features and long blonde hair peered at Rache with something bordering on sympathy.

"Can we go somewhere private to talk?" she asked conspiratorially.

"I'm not going anywhere with you until you explain what you want. There's nobody around here," stated Rache.

"If I can find you, so can they," the strange woman uttered quietly.

"They? Getting a bit paranoid here, aren't we?"

This woman knows me or about me from my timeline, not yours. She may well have been the one taking pot-shots at you...us, this afternoon. Get rid of her.

"Not half as paranoid as either you or I should be. You are in grave danger. I have some answers for you. Like the memory gaps."

That caught their attention. If the handsome woman knew something about the missing memories, she may prove beneficial to them. Rizzo was instructing Rache through the different outcomes of different scenarios.

"What's your name and how do you know about me or Dr Rizzoli?" Rache asked.

Sighing, "My name is Cordelia Maynard in this timeline. Dr Rizzoli doesn't know me. We've never met. However, I have close contact with...relatives of Dr Rizzoli from her timeline in UCA."

"Bullshit! My dad has passed and my mother is borderline dementia. I have no siblings or aunts and uncles. I have no relatives, Miss Maynard."

"Not yet, no."

The exploding monitor in front of Rache and Cordelia startled them both, causing them to duck below the desk lines.

"You brought them here?"

"No, no, I swear. I knew it wouldn't be long though. We have to get out of here. I have a car waiting out the back. If we crawl along this row until we reach the end, we can get to the nearest bookshelves. If we run straight down that aisle, we come to a wall. At the far left will be an emergency exit to a rear lane. Go," she ordered.

Rachelle Shaw did not have time to argue or debate the issues. She knew that danger was present. She had narrowly missed being shot several times already in just one day. A thousand and one questions assaulted her weary brain as she crawled swiftly across the carpeted floor, thankful for the jeans she wore protecting her knees. The other woman, Cordelia, was close on her heels. Now, Rachelle Shaw had a time traveller in her head and one behind her in the form of a physical person. The endless day was morphing into a nightmare or a fantasy; she wasn't sure which.

The emergency alarms were activated the second the lever of the rear door was pushed down to release the escapees into the night. Cordelia ushered Rache along the alley to a waiting EV. Although a relatively cheap vehicle, it had a decent enough power train to get away quickly and quietly. Rache was shoved roughly through the door once the woman opened it for her with a remote fob.

"We need to get to my motel room," Rache gushed breathlessly once Cordelia had taken up position in the driver's side. Rache had been in one or two autonomous vehicles but never one without a steering wheel."

"State the address," instructed the voice.

Rache obeyed the instructions, speaking aloud the name of the motel where she was staying. The car leapt into action immediately purring out of the alley silently, turning right after indicating dutifully and merging with the city traffic. The metallic female voice provided the vehicle's occupants with an estimated time of arrival at their destination.

"We won't be able to stay there."

Rache was informed by her 'rescuer'?

"I paid for a week in advance," protested Rache. "I gave up something very precious to me to get the money."

"You have no idea what you gave up for this jaunt."

"Fill me in then would you"

"Not yet, not fully, at least. I have to prepare you for the complete picture."

How does this Amazonian know me? I don't know her from a bar of soap.

"How do you know...Rizzo?"

"Rizzo? So, she isn't with you, then? If she was, she would murder someone before allowing them to call her that! Damn! It didn't work at all then...but, you said..."

"She's here, alright. She's in my goddam head and I hate this shit. What the fuck is this all about and why am I in danger?"

"I was afraid of that. The transfer didn't take properly because of the incorrect mapping procedures and the...other thing."

"Can none of you twerps from the future just answer a simple question? Everything you guys say has one big, cliffhanging ending.

Start afresh. What went wrong with the mapping procedure?"

"It's supposed to happen with a fully cognisant patient. If the brain is not at that level of consciousness, it creates an anomaly in the coding and the uptake. If Dr Rizzoli had been conscious when they mapped her brain, the transfer would have taken place instantly. Without that, it will take time for the transfer to complete the takeover."

"No shit. It's started, though. She has control of my lower body. We have to concentrate hard on coordinating our efforts just to achieve crawling and walking. Crawling, we learned the hard way."

"Wait a minute. Are you...in communication with her?"

"Yeah, so?"

"No one thought of that possibility. So, Dr Rizzoli is in there with you and you two can speak with one another?"

Sighing, "Yeah, she's there, alright. Bloody pain in the butt, but she's there."

Shut-up.

"You shut up!"

"Sorry?" asked Cordelia.

"Not you, her."

"She told you to shut up?"

"First she wants me to communicate then she wants me to shut up. This weird-arse day just can't get any weirder or worse."

"I'm afraid that's not true," warned Cordelia.

"Yeah, right. Assassins and all that? Well, I know about that already."

"That isn't the worst."

"Oh, get real. What could be worse than someone trying to end your life?"

"Someone ending the lives of the ones you hold nearest and dearest is way worse."

"Make some sense, would you?" demanded Rache observing the cityscape passing by them as the silent car whisked them through the busy streets. "I told you, I don't have anyone that is 'nearest and dearest' to me."

"And I responded to that with a 'not yet'."

"What does that mean?"

"Your children. Your two wonderful children who haven't been born yet. Gabrielle and Lorenzo Rizzoli, born one year apart beginning with Gabs around a year from now."

The agonising scream from within her head caused Rache to falter, placing her hands on either side of her head to keep from collapsing. Her brain swam and her vision starred with tears obscuring her sight. Inside, Rache felt as if a harpoon had entered her chest. The massive pain threatened to cause a pulmonary episode. Rache clutched her chest with the waves of agony coursing over her. Worse still than the physical jolt was the mental anguish attempting to drown her in misery and grief. Unable to cope with the strain, Rache blacked out.

TEN

The squawk of seagulls penetrated the fug clouding her thoughts. Morning sunlight shone through the clean window pane and the filmy curtains. Rache was in a room that screamed young girl, with everything coloured in varying shades of pink and musk. A gentle sea breeze, flavoured with salt and another tangy, unidentifiable source, wafted gently through the open sash window on the other side of the room. A single fly buzzed annoyingly overhead.

Gradually, Rache came around to greet the new day with a mixture of concern and grief that knew no bounds. It made her body ache inside like it had lost a vital organ. Though the trauma was not hers, understanding that the feelings mostly emanated from her passenger, she felt it just the same. It was a debilitating feeling of total loss and grief like she had never experienced before, even when her father passed.

Rache had not experienced childbirth or the inextricable bond between a mother and child, yet wasn't able to shake the deep melancholia sweeping over her. Her guest it seemed, had borne children in Rache's future. Two, if Cordelia's information was correct. Something happened to them in Rizzo's timeline, possibly without her knowledge. No, that couldn't be right. Rizzo had to have known for the news to have such a devastating impact on her.

Rache had never contemplated having children. Her vocation was too important to her. The world in which she lived wasn't suitable for new life and part of Rache's ambition was to help with that state of affairs. At least, from an energy perspective.

There was no sign of her interloper when she rose to sit on the edge of the bed with a weary body. It came as a shock to realise that she had control of her lower portions again. The frilly pink bedcover tickled her calves, confirming that her legs were her own. Distant sounds of surf and seagulls washed over her as Rache became aware of her surroundings. Pleasant sounds of the beach. So relaxing and peaceful at other times when the weight of the world and the future of all humanity were not resting on the shoulders of one woman.

It took some time for Rache to notice the small face peering around the doorframe, staring at her shyly.

"Hello there. Is this your beautiful room?" she asked in her kindest tone. The young girl of no more than ten nodded, with a smile forming on her full lips. "What's your name?"

The girl ran off in a mild panic, having been taught well by her mother not to talk to strangers. Cordelia approached soon after to stand at the doorway.

"Good morning. I hope you managed to get some sleep?"

"Sort of," replied Rache, feeling every bone, muscle and sinew in her aching body.

"Coffee?"

"I could die for a cup," said Rache with a heavy sigh.

"How is..."

"Rizzo?"

"She really lets you call her that?"

"She suggested it. To keep us apart she said she would call me Rache and I should call her Rizzo."

"Well, anyone calling her anything but Dr Rizzoli in the future would cop such an earful that they would regret it. I'll stick to calling her that if she's available?"

"Not a boo from her since you delivered the bombshell. Not even sure she's still there. Where are we?"

"Woody Point. Part of the Redcliffe Peninsula. Come on, we'll get you something to eat and a cuppa."

"Was that your daughter before?" asked Rache as she made her way through the bungalow towards the kitchen at the rear, feeling manky from sleeping in her clothes from the previous night.

"Yes, Molly. She came and told me you were awake. She's having her cereal before going off to a friend's house for a play date."

"No school?"

"Saturday."

"Oh, yeah, I forgot."

Rache settled herself at the laminated table with retro colours and patterns. A cup of coffee awaited her while Cordelia set about frying up some eggs. Molly watched on in silent curiosity.

"So, how did you know Rizzo?"

"I didn't. I worked with her daughter Gabs. I was her supervisor. I'm a botanist and horticulturist. That's how I earned my ticket to UCA."

"UCA?"

"You don't know much, do you? Under-City Australis."

"That would be just U.A. then?"

"Yep, you're Dr Rachelle Rizzoli alright. Bit of a stickler I was told. I believe she went right off the reservation when America announced its undercity name as Under-Sity America, with an 'S' instead of a 'C'."

"Oh, I get it, still the USA, huh? Trust them."

"How do you like your eggs?"

"Oh, I'm not hungry..."

"Tough! You need to eat. Look, Rachelle, whether you realise it or not, you have a monumental task ahead. It's bigger than any individual or even country. Dr Rizzoli has to save the human race from extinction."

"Should we be talking about this...?" Rache enquired with a pointing of the head towards Molly.

"Molly knows. When I came back I told her straight away."

"Why are you back?"

"You won't like the answer."

"Me, or..."

"Dr Rizzoli. Not you so much."

"Well?"

"I was sent back to make sure Dr Rizzoli failed in her mission by any means necessary."

"Why?"

"I don't know. I was never given a reason and I didn't need one."

"So everything you've said to us so far is a lie?" asked Rache feeling nervous.

"Relax, no. I only volunteered for one reason; Molly."

"Huh?"

"I would've said or done anything for the chance to get back to my little girl."

"She was with you in that underground city, wasn't she?"

"No. I was tricked. I earned my place in the city and was told they were making arrangements for Molly and my mother to join me in a couple of days. UCA was locked down that night and the entrance was blocked by armed guards. I know, I argued till I was blue in the face with them to let me through. They stood there like robots. They threatened to shoot me if I persisted in my attempts to break through their cordon."

"That's awful."

"Mine is just one story in a thousand. Everyone had to leave loved ones behind. It was a black day in human history when they shut the doors on the remaining Australians left topside to suffer a horrible death. Luckily there was no one at the entrance to see us go down. The facility's location was kept top-secret with only a handful of people knowing its whereabouts."

"What about the construction workers who built the place?"

"Every worker was offered a single place in UCA for one member of their family. That bought them the silence they needed. No one was allowed to leave the site once they began work and all communications with the rest of Australia were blocked. A few tried to break the rules and were tossed into solitary confinement topside with the offer of a ticket withdrawn."

"That's..."

"Necessary. UCA could only hold so many humans. Every lottery winner was notified in person by an officer who picked them up and took them away immediately without stopping for anything. No clothes, no goodbyes, no personal mementos, nothing. Anyone resisting was given zero opportunity to speak, with an alternate chosen from a list of nearby residents once they were locked up. Only preselected essential citizens like Dr Rizzoli and I were allowed to take a few things with us."

"Wow! So it was all real, then? What Rizzo said about the end of the world and all that?"

"Absolutely. It all ends, all life as we know it falls apart the moment the doomsday device triggers the ring of fire to blow. Within six months the entire globe was blanketed in ash and fumes. The caustic air would strip away your lungs in no time at all if you weren't wearing a proper gas mask. The sun was hidden behind the plumes of black ash for months on end, wiping out all life that depended on it very quickly.

"The undercities were planned and constructed in record time to house the lucky few, with the hope of rebuilding humanity once the air cleared. Only, no one knew exactly when that might be. Fifty to a hundred years was the optimistic opinion doing the rounds. No one really knew. When sounds from topside were monitored and interpreted as survivors digging towards the city, they detonated tonnes of rubble to fill the tunnels on top of the entrance. UCA was blocked off to the topside for the foreseeable future. Another dark day for us all. Life went on. We worked at our assigned tasks to sustain life underground. None of it could have happened without Dr Rachelle Rizzoli. If she hadn't broken the law by meddling with the doomsday device, no one would have had the wherewithal to provide the geothermal energy required to power a city underground."

Yeah, they arrested and tried me for it in a kangaroo court where they found me not guilty on most charges. Some fucking gratitude.

"Rizzo?"

"Is she back?" asked Cordelia.

Rache nodded. Molly looked confused, peering from her mother to the other woman and wondering who it was that had arrived. "Dr Rizzoli, I need to explain a few things if you'll let me?"

"I wouldn't wait for an answer if I were you," advised Rache.

"Dr Rizzoli, I was approached anonymously about a chance to go back to my younger self, on the proviso that I undertake a mission to stop you."

So, she's the assassin?

"Rizzo wants to know if that makes you the assassin."

"In their eyes, yes. In reality, never. Remember I was with you in the library when you were shot at. I accepted the mission to get back to my daughter, Molly, who never made it with me into UCA. I would have given up anything for that opportunity, or at least, appear to. The mission was to stop you at all costs."

Why, for fuck's sake?

"Um, she wants to know why."

"I never knew. Only, when I got here and started thinking about it, I got angry. If you could do what they sent you to do, then it seemed incredibly stupid to thwart that opportunity. I decided to find you and warn you. Molly, if you've finished your breakfast, I'd like you to head over to Kathy's place for your play date."

"Okay, Mummy."

Molly took off excitedly down the hall with her plaited pigtails bouncing, exiting the front door. The door banged shut with the help of the wind. Cordelia winced.

"Not sure how many times I have to ask her to close a door gently," she sighed.

"It seems like a total conflict of interest for anyone from your timeline to want to stop Rizzo here. Of what possible benefit would it be...to anyone?"

"I haven't been able to figure that one out, which is why I became so angry after arriving here. Seeing that sun out there again, despite all the problems the world faced, forced me to get in touch with you. Even though every ounce of me just wanted to enjoy this time with my daughter and forget everything else. I have no idea who contacted me or their motives. I intend to assist you in every way possible to achieve your mission. That little girl out there is worth fighting for, whatever we're up against."

Ask her how many others have been sent back that she knows of and if she thinks there were any failed missions.

Cordelia thought about the question after Rache relayed Rizzo's enquiry.

"I came past a room in the area I was taken to containing two beds with two patients. They were hooked up to monitors and had all kinds of tubes running in and out of them. The doctor who took charge of me admitted that they were failures. In as much as they could determine seeing as no information could be brought forward from the past. The best they could figure is that something occurred to them in the past which rendered them vegetative. They died a few hours after I arrived.

"Something else made me angry, though, even before I arrived here. Dr Rizzoli's daughter and I became very close from the moment she came to work for me. I became a surrogate mother, of sorts for Gabs, and she, a daughter for me. She confided everything to me, everything. I was told of the offer made to Dr Rizzoli and the dilemma she faced as a result. It was an untenable position to place her in, making her choose between her children and saving the world. Even worse, that one of the directors had been to see both the children to engage their support.

"The decision for me to return was an easy one because I would be reunited with my daughter. Dr Rizzoli faced the prospect of not only abandoning her children to an unknown fate but possibly eradicating them from our timeline if she wasn't able to reproduce them in the past. They could have ended up like those two vegetables I saw, or worse.

"The pressure on Dr Rizzoli was pure torture for her and the children. When she refused to comply with their wishes, the pressure was increased on the children. So much so that they ended up taking their own lives to relieve their mother of the decision. Without them in the picture Dr Rizzoli would be free to do the right thing, to save everyone. The Council never figured out the effect the tragedy would have on the mother. Normally seen as a woman of steel, Dr Rizzoli broke down entirely.

"I was in the mapping area several days after the tragedy when they brought her in on a stretcher, mumbling incoherently. I watched them begin the mapping process after they sedated her. I knew enough about the procedure by then to realise that it would be detrimental to Doctor Rizzoli, if not lethal, to send her back in that condition. When I objected strongly, I was given the assurance that they would remove those memories of the tragedy from her files. I didn't think such a horrible thing was possible. I can see it's true, though by what I see and hear now from you. I am so, so sorry, Dr Rizzoli."

"We both knew something was wrong. I felt it just as much as Rizzo. They may have removed the memories but not the emotions surrounding them. Rizzo felt the pain of it coursing through our minds and in my heart, I felt the worst kind of ache. You are the worst kind of callous shits in the future. How could anyone do that to her, a cripple who went through ten kinds of hell and ended up saving the fucking lot of you? It's despicable, unconscionable."

"We aren't all like that, Rachelle. I promise we aren't all like that. I felt so bad for that, Dr Rizzoli, I truly did. I heard all about you through Gabs and I couldn't help but feel for your pain. Fortunately, I thought I could do more to help you here than there, which is why I volunteered for the mission. I want to help you stop this...cataclysm, if possible."

"Rizzo says that theoretically, it shouldn't be possible. Altering the past merely delays and or shifts the pattern of incidents."

"I've heard all the arguments for and against. I don't see that there is another option. If we try and fail, we're no worse off. Did you have a plan?"

Don't tell her! All this may be a ruse to get us onside so she can deliver the coup d'état. She admitted to taking on the mission and this could be her way of delivering on that deal. One is sent back to assassinate; another is sent back to try other methods. Sure, it's all cutesy with the daughter and such. Great sob story if you believe it. Well, I don't and if you do, you're a bigger sap than I imagined.

Rache decided not to tell Cordelia about Rizzo's suspicions. That was something she'd keep to herself for the time being. It was very convenient that Cordelia happened to show up at just the right time in the library. She could be in league with the assassin, arranging it to look like she becomes the heroine rescuing Rachelle in the nick of time.

"Rizzo had a couple of ideas floating around her head but nothing specific," Rache lied.

Cordelia picked up on the hesitation immediately, though chose to ignore it. It was a delicate situation and she understood completely if she weren't fully trusted by either woman just yet. She would have to relegate herself to second fiddle for the time being offering what assistance she could to achieve their goals.

Rachelle pecked at the eggs on toast placed before her, while Cordelia busied herself tidying up. It was clear to Rachelle that if she was in any danger from the woman, she could have been dispatched already. That didn't suggest she should place a whole heap of trust in her either. Before any more thoughts could surface, Rachelle face-planted her eggs.

"Are you alright?" Cordelia asked as she lifted Rache's face from the plate of eggs.

"Jeez, if you're going to take over my functions, would you at least do so competently?"

"You're talking to Dr Rizzoli right now, right?"

"Yeah, I just lost control of my upper half. I felt the loss of my legs when Rizzo came back just before. Now she seems to have control of it all except my face. Fuck! I don't want to fade away to nothing," said Rache with panic in her voice, scraping eggs and butter off her face.

Don't be such a baby. I didn't know it was going to happen.

Cordelia smiled but sympathised to a certain extent, "You do live on, you know?"

"Where's your younger self?"

"Point taken," Cordelia admitted.

"There's nothing left of her, is there?"

"A mere echo, I'm afraid. It wasn't supposed to happen that way for you. Nobody could have predicted what would happen if the transfer didn't take immediately. Whatever my younger person was thinking before I took over is gone completely, thank goodness. Not sure I could have coped with what you're experiencing. It can't be good for either of you."

"You have no idea."

Bitch, bitch, moan, whinge. We have a deadline to meet in case you forgot. And you have a date.

Rache had no idea what Rizzo meant by her last statement. A date? Who the fuck was she going to date and why would she do so at a time like the present?

Because you have babies to make. I just found out my children are dead so we have to make them again.

"Are you out of your fucking mind?!" Rache blurted out suddenly.

"What?" asked Cordelia instinctively clutching her breast at the outburst.

"Not you."

"How can I tell?"

"Fair call. I need some time alone with you know who. I'll go for a walk on the beach so you won't get confused. If she cooperates, that is."

Rache stood suddenly, like a puppet master had pulled her strings, only her arms hung limply by her sides. She stood swaying as if drunk.

"Are you..."

"No, I'm not alright. I don't know if either one of us has control of my arms, which makes balancing very hard."

"How on earth do you think you're going to manage crossing several streets to get to the beach?"

"We'll work on it. I'll see you later."

"What are you doing?" asked Rache once they'd reached the beach without too much fuss.

Jeez, what does it look like? I'm running.

"Yeah, I get that. I guess I meant, why are you running?"

Because I can, my dear, because I can. I haven't had this sort of freedom of movement for a long, long time. I'd forgotten how good it felt to be whole and vital. Christ, I don't even have saggy tits anymore and even my fanny feels taut and terrific. First time in ages I felt I could do anything active without the fear of bladder leakage.

"Eew! That's just gross!"

"Yeah, not pleasant. Kids have that effect on the plumbing...I guess. Get used to it, that's our main aim now."

"What about Jekyll and Hyde?"

Robert's a problem. Not a deterrence if I handle it differently.

"Thought you..." Rache ran out of breath. "Stop, okay, just...stop."

Rache collapsed onto the sand on the deserted beach peering out on Moreton Bay with Moreton Island on the horizon. A gentle breeze washed a few frothy waves ashore on the dirty sand.

"Thought you...said you hated him?" asked Rache once she caught her breath.

It doesn't matter how I feel. This is about bringing my children back to life.

"Children you don't know, have no recollection of. Children that can never be the same no matter how accurately you repeat the actions of your past?"

That's the hidden beauty of this, don't you see? It doesn't matter if they're slightly different now, because I don't have current memories of them, only the knowledge I just gained and the emotions surrounding them.

"Ergo it doesn't matter who the father is this time around either," debated Rache

Why are you resisting this? You said you fancied him and I picked up on the warmth passing through your groin at the mere sight of him.

"I could never go for a bloke that abuses females and children. Find someone else if you plan to go ahead with this insane quest. While I still have control over my mouth I won't be cooperating with you. I'll tell the scumbag coward exactly what I think of him if I come across him again."

He hasn't started that behaviour yet. It only begins once he's famous and on the road with his band touring the major cities. He takes up drugs and alcohol. That's when it begins. Before then, great sex and happy times...mostly.

"Mostly?"

There were arguments.

"Over?"

Usual shit, I suppose. I can't even remember. Money mostly, I reckon.

"Thought you said you were swimming in money?"

After. Yeah after he got well known, with their records selling and the tours sold out.

"I can't believe you're even contemplating this after what you told me."

We don't have time to find another Mr Right. We were compatible sexually, and we produced children successfully. I will do whatever it takes to bring them back into being even though I can't picture their faces anymore. I feel them. I have recollections of carrying them, of giving birth. That's where the memories fade and the emotions come alive.

"Don't we have bigger fish to fry?"

What's it all for if not for them? The next generation and the one after that. It's all pointless otherwise.

"Oh, I get that. It doesn't have to be about *your* children, though. It doesn't have to be about them. We could do this for all the others, for the future of..."

Oh puh-lease! Save me that altruistic garbage. I had enough of that crap shoved down my throat by...somebody.

"Somebody?"

Another gap in the memory. The person or persons responsible for the death of my children and my ending up here against my wishes. I never signed their bloody paperwork, their contract. I never agreed to have my brain mapped. I was brain-raped. I was told that a complete mapping would render the patient an imbecile or close to it. It was an extraction rather than a mapping. I was told my body would be euthanised after the extraction took place.

A building wind whisked the salty aroma of the sea into Rachelle's face, as well as the tangy odour she failed to identify earlier. Rotting seaweed and pollution provided the answer. The beach was littered with the detritus of civilisation in the form of plastic, plastic and more plastic. The sand was infused with millions of bits of plastic that had a few hundred years left before they broke down completely from the specks of colour they were at present. Plastic bottles and styrene containers oozing the rotting leftovers of takeaway meals made up for the majority of the rest.

Not for the first time did Rizzo wonder at the futility of her mission. It was difficult to understand the exact reason the planet should be 'saved' at all. If she thought about it logically, the planet would be better saved by eradicating humans and their destructive nature. The globe could certainly use a wholesome cleansing, wiping out all present life to begin again about a million or a billion years in the future.

"It's not that bad," said Rache.

Bullshit! It's a fucking pigsty. We messed up this planet for our future generations and I'm supposed to help with that? That sun sure is nice, though. There may be some smog in the air but it's nothing compared to the ash. Five hundred or more volcanoes all spewing out their lethal mixture into the air at once. That shit blanketed the entire Earth, including the poles, turning that once pristine white landscape into a moonscape.

"Are you going to go ahead with it or not?"

I'm not seeing the point anymore. When I first became aware of being here, I had an overriding impulse to do just that, make it right. Now, I'm not so sure.

"What about the plan involving your children? Do I get any say in that, by the way? I wasn't planning on children in my life any time soon."

It could work, now that I have no memories of the two I left behind, only the feelings attached to that. It wouldn't be a bother if they differed greatly from the originals.

"Right, but here's the thing, I don't want anything to do with that monster. Find someone else."

He only turns into a monster later. We could prevent that from happening, make sure he keeps away from drugs and booze.

"You could go back to him? After all that...animal did to you?"

For the sake of my children, yes. There is no sacrifice a mother won't make for her children. Oh, I wouldn't put up with any sort of abuse from him or anyone else. I learned a few moves that would keep me safe, especially now that I have a healthy, strong body again. No bloody crutches, no leg braces, no constant, debilitating pain. I don't miss that shit.

"I still don't understand that you could even think of going back to him."

Like I said, we can't be choosy. Time is running out. I was supposed to meet him again only a couple of days from now after a pub gig.

"What about that invite to a private night of classics?"

Oh, give me a break. He's a metalhead, a rocker, not some sort of classic musician, not a Franz Liszt at any rate. When you see him on stage you'll get it. He was hot, that's for sure. It's what drew me to him.

"What about my job? I have to go back to the flat to get my mail and pick up the threads of my life again."

Getting shot is on that agenda, is it? Don't you get it? There is no going back. I think the only way to forge ahead is to go with my original plan. Draw up the schematics and the coding for the laser drill and deliver that to Dr Thoms.

"That idea was pretty much vetoed, wasn't it? Something about our archaic computers?"

I think I can build a computer for us. I got to know enough about programming to wangle my way. I could just come up with my own software to design the damn thing. You have enough money left over to get the parts I'd need.

"That would blow the last of it. My daddy's nugget."

Can you think of a better cause on which to spend the money?

"You just said it was all pointless before. I wish you'd make up your mind."

"Yeah make up your mind lady," sneered a passer-by walking his dog.

Rache watched the gruff old man walk on, her face turning a shade of red.

What do you care what the old fart thinks of you?

"I must sound like some crazy bag lady talking to myself like that."

You're talking to me.

"Like I said, talking to myself."

Ha, ha!

Rache looked around to make sure she was alone, "I need a shower. No wonder that bloke thought I was a bit of a loony. I smell like a bum. "

We need to get away from here.

"You don't trust Cordelia?"

Not as far as I can throw her. I don't trust anyone, not even my younger self. I never realised what a flake I was.

"Just remember that you have to rely on me to talk your way into or out of situations for the time being!"

Come on then, let's have that shower and freshen up a little. I can't use your olfactory senses yet but you did look rough when I spied you in that window pane this morning. You should eat something more as well.

"Don't start trying to play mother with me."

Old habits...

Rache rose from the sand, brushing down her jeans. One last look at the oily ocean cemented a notion in Rizzo's head at least, that they should get away to be somewhere on their own. Cordelia could easily be playing a good cop, bad cop routine with them. Save them from the assassin to get in their good books then pounce when they were unaware. What Cordelia hoped to gain in such a scenario escaped Rizzo for the time being.

Moving Rache's body around was becoming almost second nature to Rizzo, while Rache, who still retained use of her arms, swung them easily with each stride. It no longer seemed the effort it was previously for either of them. Rache attempted to ignore the nagging question of how long she would continue to exist. It troubled her more than she was willing to admit. While it didn't make sense in one way, seeing as she would continue to exist in a physical capacity, she felt a deep sadness at the thought of no longer taking a conscious part in life.

Everything happened so quickly that Rache had hardly been able to digest any of it properly. Her scientific brain and febrile imagination revelled in the possibilities of it all. Time travel! It was a secret fascination of hers for as long as she could remember. Well, time travel in a more traditional sense, at least, as in a whole person being sent back or forward. Then the other aspect of throwing an old mind back into a younger body. Who hadn't dreamed of that at some point or another, wishing it could happen? Making amends for past mistakes...

"Listen, Rizzo. Forgetting about me for a moment and just concentrating on you. You've been given the opportunity of a lifetime, even though it came at a huge cost and totally against your will. I mean, being given the chance to go back and make changes on, not just a global scale, but also a personal level, is something dreams are made of. Even me, knowing what I know now, would love to go back and correct a few things from my past, like when I told Dad I wasn't going on his fossicking trips anymore. Or giving Mum such a hard time, especially after Daddy died.

"You can't repeat the past by going back to the man that ruined your lives. Not just yours but your children's. You think you can prevent his bad habits. How many women have said that before you? How many women thought they could change the man they fell in love with, the rebel, the strong virulent man they saw them as? They failed, Rizzo. Every last one of them. A leopard doesn't change its spots. Sooner or later that hidden personality, that propensity to addiction will surface.

"Besides, you know as well as I do that the exact conditions and circumstances can't be repeated to bring about the same children, or even close. I know you can't remember them as they were. You were robbed of that, I get it. That doesn't mean you should try to bring other children into the world to suffer under the tyranny of that monster...with my body! I'm not ready to have children. I have a career."

You won't have a damn thing when the planet erupts. Not a career, not a future, not a planet to live on. I agree to a certain extent about the children. It seems selfish for me to think like that. All I can say in my defence is, it must be my motherly instincts which are so deeply ingrained that they could never hope to wipe them from my mind.

"I don't get that. When did it happen that you became all maternal and shit? Because I'm not and I don't see it happening any time soon."

Probably when they were born. I don't know. It's there though. Undeniably there. I always loved the name Gabriella when I first heard that name. I wonder why I changed to Gabrielle. I suppose it was to tone down the Italian connection a bit. I guess he and his family had the final say on Lorenzo's name.

"Where are we going and what are going to do, Rizzo? Can we get your mind back to here and now? Where are my feet taking me...us?"

I've been thinking about this all wrong. Trying to build a computer and writing the software required for the complex schematics of the laser drill is not only immensely time consuming, but it may also be beyond my skill level. I was always more of a hands-on person anyway. Leaning towards practice rather than theory.

"Meaning?"

We need to build a better mousetrap. It's time to buy a cheap car and go shopping.

ELEVEN

Cordelia was more than upset when Rache returned from her walk on the beach. When she was informed that her guest was preparing to leave her house to fend for herself without revealing the plan she had in mind, Cordelia reminded her of the great risks she had taken to save her.

The anger and frustration on Cordelia's face seemed genuine, though Rache couldn't be sure how much of it was because she refused to accept any more help, or Cordelia's plans were set asunder by the decision. It was a telling moment to see how far her 'rescuer' would go to keep Rache around. Guilt assailed her as she argued her points to the woman. If it was all on the up and up, then she was slapping the woman in the teeth for risking her life. On the other hand...

Rizzo managed to convince her younger self to listen to her wise counsel. It paid to be cautious, even at the risk of offending Cordelia. The woman would have to understand that her admission left a whole lot of room for doubt. She was sent back to stop Rizzo, even though she tried to explain her way out of it. True or false, it left them with a choice to make and trust wasn't going to win over suspicion.

Rache and her 'passenger' showered and spent the rest of the morning making purchases big and small. The cheap car that was purchased, a very old hybrid type from the days before fuel-reliant cars were outlawed, managed to barely get them around the suburbs, wheezing and panting like an old man with emphysema.

After the shopping was complete, including some new clothes, they made their way along the Bruce Highway towards Burpengary, a northern suburb of Brisbane. Rizzo had a hunch about somewhere they could stay. When Dr Thoms was based in Brisbane, he'd taken his class on a field trip out past Caboolture to a place somewhere before Kingaroy. Before the bus had taken the eager students back to inner Brisbane, they'd stopped off at a small shack Dr Thoms owned in the back of Burpengary.

Rache and Rizzo both knew of the place and agreed it was a good choice, knowing Dr Thoms would not be there and also knowing where the spare key was kept. It also housed all the facilities they required for their project. Dr Thoms had made a respectable laboratory within the shack to accommodate his extracurricular experiments with all kinds of inventions, fanciful and otherwise.

Though the concept of a laser drill was never mentioned to Rache in her dealings with Dr Thoms, Rizzo knew about his leanings in that area, even that early on, from what she remembered of his bedside vigils. It was very strange for Rache to become aware of conversations she'd never had or experiences in which she had yet to participate, through her passenger.

The 'shack' was substantially more than what Rizzo or Rache remembered. They concluded that improvements had been made from the last time they were there. The key, however, was in the same place, albeit a different key to a vastly different door. From the outside, it appeared to be no more than a basic high-set Queenslander with wide verandas on all four sides. Underneath the house was mostly walled in and given over to the extensive laboratory. The door, only able to be accessed from the interior of the house was dead-bolted. It took Rizzo only moments to find the key beneath a dying, potted monstera deliciosa.

Rizzo mentally kicked herself upon entering Dr Thoms' laboratory. Almost all the components purchased on their shopping spree were duplicated within the lab. She should have known that Dr Thoms would have the major components to the drill. All that was needed was to piece them together in the correct order and write the software to achieve his purpose, something he most likely hadn't completed.

Rizzo moved through the small lab with a sense of awe, knowing that a momentous scientific development would occur there in the very near future. A new thought began to form. Originally, she had the idea of constructing a miniature prototype of the drill to gift the doctor. Seeing all the componentry required to make the full-size version, about the size of a large suitcase, scattered about her, altered her plans dramatically.

Dr Thoms was most likely to return to his weekender in a few short days. His main residence was in Brookfield, a leafy outer suburb of Brisbane to the northwest of the city centre. Rizzo also knew that her old mentor travelled extensively as part of his role. In four years, Dr Thoms would begin his experiments at the bottom of the Bougainville Trench from a deep-sea drilling platform after joining a private conglomerate. In 2150, he would unleash Armageddon. In 2155 the lottery winners would descend into the undercities around the globe, shutting their doors on the topside for the foreseeable future. A decade later Rizzo was told it would all come to an end with the failing air purifiers.

The abiding question running through Rizzo's mind was, could she prevent that from happening? Can history be changed? The science fiction community would have you believe it. The hard science community of 2165 believed it could be achieved. Rizzo feared it was inevitable that the cataclysm would occur at some point. Her logic told her that, at best, she might bring about a delay. In her Hitler analogy where the dictator is killed at birth or before, just meant that someone else takes his place, possibly someone worse. There would have been a void left to be filled in Germany at the time when Hitler came into prominence.

Rizzo was twenty-seven when she had applied for the career position within the Department of Energy, with the sole purpose of finding and producing geothermal energy for Australia. Conventional drilling could not achieve the depths required to access the deep pockets well below the Earth's crust. Tapping into the pocket and maintaining the bore's integrity presented major problems. That was eventually solved with the invention of a super-fast drying epoxy/enamel coating able to withstand the hottest temperatures known to exist in those thermal pockets. However, drilling to the required depths had all the eggheads scratching their collective noggins, including Rizzo at the time.

Reaching the steam pockets above magmatic layers deep within the mantle required a new way of thinking, which is where Dr Thoms came into his own. Of course, lasers were not new. Laser cutting tools of many types were in use across the globe in all manner of situations. Laser drilling required many elements to come together before it could even be considered. Not the least of which, was a method of controlling the incursion depths. With enough power, in theory, a laser drill could simply shoot right through the Earth. Hence the need for the all-important intensity formulae and the correlating restrictions on the laser drill.

"Doing my head in with all that thinking up there, Rizzo," said

Rache after remaining silent for a long time."

You're getting all that?

"Duh! You're in my head!"

Touché.

"So?"

So what?

"We've broken into the weekend home of our mentor, what now?"

Thought you said you got all that I was thinking from a moment ago?

"When I was paying attention. Come on, mother, cut to the chase, give me the low down."

Enough with all the old clichés. It's simple really. We build the laser drill with all the proper configurations here in his lab. When he comes back, it's here for him.

"The first thing he'll do is call the cops after he finds out his house has been broken into. The cops will confiscate anything the doctor says isn't his."

I intend to leave a note, of course. I have to explain what I did and why.

"You're going to tell him that he caused the end of the world with his original drill design?"

Not in so many words...

"Perhaps you can tell me that to my face," boomed a deep baritone voice from behind Rache.

"Fuck! Don't sneak up on a person like that."

"You're the one sneaking around my house, Rachelle Shaw! I have every right to do whatever I please in my own home."

Rache looked upon the charismatic man with deep brown eyes and a greying beard. A full head of wavy brown hair flecked with grey completed the picture of the handsome, bear of a man.

"Care to explain what you're doing breaking into my home and exactly what you were talking about and to whom?"

We're going to have to tell him the truth, I reckon.

"I...I..."

"Hardly an explanation, Miss Shaw. I thought better of your English skills. Maybe if I called the police...?"

You're going to have to say everything I tell you if we're going to avoid getting arrested.

"I have a lot to tell you, Dr Thoms, perhaps over a coffee?" suggested Rache after being prompted by Rizzo.

"You have exactly the time it takes for me to make a coffee and for us both to drink it. If I'm not satisfied with your answer, I'll have you arrested for industrial espionage as well as breaking and entering. Not here, though. Upstairs, in the kitchen, NOW!"

"Something tells me he isn't going to be very receptive to our story, Rizzo," said Rache quietly, mounting the steps to walk solemnly upwards.

"What was that?" asked Dr Thoms suspiciously.

"Talking to myself...literally," answered Rache with a sardonic smile.

Don't fuck with this man, Rache. Don't paraphrase, improvise or attempt to be funny. He's one of the smartest men I knew. He'll see through fabrication or a glib comment in a fraction of a second. Follow my script or we're both in shit.

"Okay, have a seat at the table. I'll brew us a pot of coffee. Anything else, a bite to eat, maybe watch a bit of my TV or use my Wi-Fi?"

"I wasn't trying to steal anything or spy on you, Dr Thoms. I..."

"How about we drop the title and just call me Henry. You aren't one of my students anymore. It'll be fascinating to hear you explain being in my home, and in particular, my laboratory. Go ahead and make it good. I'm not known for my patience."

Henry filled an espresso pot with coffee grounds before placing it on the gas flame. Something about his demeanour suggested a less than confrontational attitude toward Rachelle. Rizzo remarked on it to her host and began to add a few clues together. Memories of his time at her hospital bedside surfaced, revealing new snippets of information she had previously missed or purposely ignored. She gradually understood that her bitterness as she recovered from the trauma of her accident caused her to block out anything to do with relationships between a man and woman. She loathed to think of it or listen to it.

As the new thoughts filtered through to her, she came to understand some of the after-play occurring when her time in hospital had ended. The odd and awkward reactions by Dr Thoms at that time when Rizzo said a final goodbye without a thank you or kind word. His conversations with her drifted into her consciousness with newfound clarity.

She hadn't lied when she said she had no idea what the boffins were talking about or when they said that she had an 'in' with Dr Thoms because of his feelings toward her. She'd dismissed them out of hand. Now, it seemed as though Rizzo was perhaps the only person who was unaware of those unreciprocated feelings, even though he was the one to talk her out of giving up on life. Her brain would not allow her to think of anything other than friendship at the time. Her brain rebelled against manhood in general. She had decided to wipe men out of her life altogether after what she'd been through. After all, she was no longer able to attract another person with her mangled, twisted body and mind.

Over the following hour and several cups of coffee, Rache explained in great detail the series of events that led up to the moment she had been surprised by him in his laboratory. The big man looked over his horn-rimmed glasses to peer at Rachelle as if he were inspecting dirt under a fingernail.

"How can you possibly expect me to believe one word of anything you've just said?"

"By telling you something you told me...er...her, Rizzo, while she was in the hospital. You told her how your Aunty Grace used to give you...'special' showers?"

Henry almost dropped his mug at the mention of that, a secret he told no one...ever. A secret he had sworn to take to his grave. The delicious, though forbidden, memories of those times with his young aunt haunted him to the present. His father's younger step-sister played a large role in Henry's life growing up. With both his parents involved in several financial enterprises gaining them a jet-set lifestyle, their son remained at boarding school and often stayed with his aunt during the holidays.

Henry didn't make much of those 'special' sessions at the time, thinking with his nether regions rather than his brain. He supposed it might be every boy's dream to be introduced to sex in such a fashion, with an older, sexy and curvaceous woman. What it accomplished, though, was a troubling impossibility to replicate those feeling for another female closer to his age...until Rachelle Shaw had entered his classroom many, many years later, many years his junior.

Henry continued to see his aunt after graduating, though never repeating those special times. Grace and he had somehow come to an unspoken understanding that the past was to be left in the past. It didn't stop Henry from reaching an erection at the mere hint of a hug or a peck on the cheek from her. Just the whiff of her favourite perfume sent paroxysms of pure pleasure through his groin, occasionally, resulting in a need to change underwear. Henry had attained the venerable age of forty-five without finding anyone comparable to his first love until he saw...her.

He maintained a strict student-teacher relationship with Rachelle Shaw throughout their association, hiding, he believed, any signs of his affections for her. The fact that every one of his students witnessed him ogling his favourite student on many occasions never occurred to him or Rachelle, who was buried in her studies. Henry knew that a relationship with a student, though she was of consenting age, would cause him to run afoul of the Dean, possibly losing his tenure at the university.

It wasn't long until Henry had given his notice as he could no longer trust himself and had no wish to tarnish his reputation, applying for and eventually accepting a position with a private energy company.

"Who...who told you that?" Henry finally asked, placing his mug down carefully on the table.

"You did, in the hospital where you sat by Rizzo's bed for nearly a year. You told her everything about you, your life, your hopes, dreams and expectations. You explained in great detail the idea you had for a laser drill and how close you were to completion of the prototype. You also told her how much in love you were with her, and that there could be no going forward for you in a life without her in it. Rizzo wants to apologise for that, by the way."

"What do you... I mean, what does she mean by that?"

"She says she treated you abominably once she was able to talk again when all the hardware was removed from her broken jaw. She says she was too traumatised and bitter to understand what you were saying to her, to fully understand it. You were the perfect gentleman and never once pushed your agenda on her. You accepted her inability to love or even consider 'being' with a man again. You left once it was clear that she had no room for you in her heart or her home. All unsaid, of course. Understood by you, intimated by her, but never recognised until just a few moments ago when those memories started coming back to her," said Rache with sincere sadness.

Henry sat at the table ashen-faced and unable to find his voice. Rache looked at him sympathetically while reserving her own opinions on the developing scene. She admitted to having seen Dr Thoms staring at her once or twice during her classes but giving away nothing that held a clue as to his feelings for her. It all came as a bit of surprise to them both.

It was a difficult pill for Henry to swallow. A young woman for whom he'd secretly longed the moment he saw her, forcing him to give up a career he'd loved, relating a story from her future self about events that were yet to transpire. Including a secret that had never left his lips to another living soul. Damned if the story she told about him visiting the injured Rachelle Rizzoli didn't sound like something he would do if that happened to the young person he loved with all his heart.

While Rachelle Shaw had convinced his heart that she was telling the truth, she failed to convince his mind on more than one level. Most of all...

"I don't know where you obtained your information and I will find out. However, there is one serious flaw in your story."

"Just the one?" Rache asked jokingly.

Stop fucking with him! No improvising.

"I said one *serious* flaw. Other anomalies don't hold a patch to that one."

"And that is?"

"Your inflammable and insulting remark that I could employ a defective instrument."

"None of us are perfect. It could have..."

"Let me stop you right there. It isn't defective and never could be."

"Sorry, but it was. Your calculations..."

"Have been proven."

"What do you mean?"

"I mean that my device is proven to work."

"You've built the prototype already?"

"I built the prototype years ago. I have been experimenting with the actual device in a secret location for a few months now and it works fine. Of course, I haven't employed it to drill downwards yet.

I've been using it to drill horizontally through a mountain to gauge its effectiveness against different geological formations. I wouldn't have proceeded to drill into the crust or further until it was fully tested and functioning 100%. I conclude, that seeing as I gave it full power and did not shoot through the mountain that I could not have done so in the future, as you suggested. Did you really think I wouldn't have had every last line of code and the maths checked by the best and brightest?"

"That's impossible. The one thing they found when your drilling platform exploded was a bright red watertight floatation safe. The schematics for your device were in that safe. Rizzo had direct access to those files found on a memory stick. The formula used to determine the earth's density was incorrect, making the intensity limits and configurations on the drill flawed. It happened. Rizzo saw the devastating effects your device produced when it breached the core long enough for a magma plume to escape."

Huffing with impatience, Henry tore himself from the table, returning shortly afterwards to throw down a heap of well-eared papers on the table before Rachelle.

"Show me," he demanded.

Rache reluctantly picked up the sheath of papers, studying them one by one, allowing Rizzo to examine them with her. After several minutes, she lowered the papers to the table.

"Rizzo doesn't understand. She saw the schematics from the file and..."

"Are you entirely dense? Can't you see what's before you? I handwrite everything. I never committed any of the designs to a digital footprint. I even wrote the code on paper. I've done it that way all my life. Of course, the code eventually has to be transcribed onto a computer to run the device, but I never make a digital copy of the design or the code. Still haven't even though the Minister for Energy wants it before he'll commit more funds to my research. That's why I'm staying private with this. Once the government has its mitts on my design, they'll find a way to do me out of what's rightfully mine."

"It doesn't make any sense according to Rizzo. She says she saw the schematics retrieved from the flotation safe after the rescue vessel failed to find any survivors from the *Bougainville Belle*, as the drilling platform was called. As the senior geophysicist in the department at the time, it was left to her to interpret the information on that stick. Rizzo saw clearly how the formula for calculating the Earth's density had incorrect figures. Knowing how critical that information was to the laser's design, she examined the configurations included in the schematics for the design...flawed."

"Young lady, I have spent longer at this game than anyone else I know and I wouldn't even consider using the Bougainville Trench for such a hazardous experiment. I am not given to having impulsive or reckless notions. I know full-well how impossibly dangerous it would be to drill near that volatile area. Tonga was wiped out only a decade ago by that erupting volcano and the area hasn't settled yet. Only an absolute fool would..."

"What is it?" asked Rache. Henry had stopped abruptly, the colour draining from his face.

"The Minister for Energy, his PA mentioned the trench... Can't recall that man's name. A namby-pamby sort of fellow. Wishy-washy was my first impression of him, high speaking voice and dressed almost identically to the Minister. I wasn't listening to what was being said at the time. I did overhear mention of the Bougainville Trench as a possible drilling site. One that I immediately dismissed in my mind but perhaps not out loud. My mind was on many things at the time, and the conversation was not meant for my ears presumably."

"So, how could you have ended up on that drilling platform if you were so adamant about it being too risky a location?"

"How am I supposed to answer to an accusation on future events? This is absurd. I have no idea why I'm entertaining you in this manner, Miss Shaw."

"Rache, call me Rache. She does."

"This is impossible. You call her Rizzo and she calls you Rache?"

"We can't keep calling each other by the same name. It's too confusing" Rache shrugged.

"Maybe we should go to the authorities with..."

"Are you kidding? If I can't get you to believe me, how could I possibly convince anyone else? And, it probably isn't safe."

"Meaning?"

"Creating too much attention will give the assassin access to us."

"Sorry? What assassin?"

"Didn't we mention that bit? Rizzo says it looks like someone else has been sent back in time to stop her."

"Wouldn't that be rather counter-productive?"

"You'd think so, wouldn't you? Rizzo can't think of a single reason why anyone would want to stop the end of the world. Not that she believes in her mission at any rate. Something about fate and paradoxes and such."

"All theoretical and hard to prove since no one would know if it was accomplished."

"Exactly! That's what she said. Doctor...Henry? Did you really leave university because of me? I wondered what happened to you."

Embarrassed and blushing, the florid-faced doctor found no easy way out of answering, "Ah, yes, I'm ashamed to say."

"Ashamed?"

You need to stop this line of questions. We need him on our side.

"I am many years your senior and it would have been entirely inappropriate for me to pursue my feelings at the time."

"And now?"

Knock it off, bimbo! Get your thoughts out of your knickers. I can feel the heat up here.

"Now, I am still your senior by a good many years. That hasn't changed."

"Do you still have feelings toward me?"

"I haven't called the police yet."

"STOP!"

"What?" asked Henry in mild panic at the sudden outburst.

What just happened?

"Rache? I'm...speaking...out loud?"

Rizzo?

"Looks like I've taken over the voice box. Hi Henry, I'm Dr Rachelle Rizzoli from the year 2165. I'm 47 years old and was living in Under-City Australis, several kilometres beneath what was left of Canberra. It's been so good catching up with you after everything you did for me. Once again, I have to apologise for my behaviour and ingratitude."

"So, I'm no longer speaking to Rachelle Shaw?"

"Doesn't appear so, no. I can hear her in my head, though. Or did. Silent as the grave up there now. Probably because she was such an air-head. I cannot believe how immature I was back then. You know, you have this image of yourself and you feel all superior and shit, but it's all a disguise meant to impress others."

Bitch!

"Okay, there we go. No, not alone, she's still there with that charming mouth of hers. No manners or respect at all for her elders."

Henry witnessed the altered tones, inflections and body language that transformed his former student in the blink of an eye. It didn't seem possible that anyone could achieve that if they were play-acting. It was clear, instantly, that he was dealing with a more mature person than before. He wasn't able to pinpoint the reason he believed that exactly, but it was evident. The tall tale related to him just increased its validity in his mind. Or it might be that he had been fooled into believing it by some incredible acting skills.

He didn't know what to think anymore. So much of what she said was impossible in so many ways. Not the least of which were the claims of his defective laser drill becoming a doomsday device. Utter madness, the whole thing, he thought as he shook his head in consternation. In the back of his mind, however, nagged the nuances of odd behaviours exhibited during his recent meetings with the Department of Energy, especially the fellow following the Minister around like a lap dog.

Henry began to wonder how secure his test site was. Only he and two other people knew about it, neither of whom held his complete trust. Not that either person had all the information. Henry had been very circumspect in revealing only patches of information or wads of formulas to persons, prohibiting any general knowledge of the overall project. Everyone received only a small piece of the puzzle so that no one could assimilate or connect it to any known projects or papers of his. Yet, it was not an impossibility that he'd been spied on, or been...

"Damn!" he said suddenly.

"What is it?"

"I haven't scanned the lab lately or checked the hidden CCTV feeds in quite a while.

Half an hour later, they had found a total of five listening devices planted in very good places throughout the lab. The CCTV footage also revealed an earlier break-in by a masked intruder placing the bugs and recording everything within the lab, taking pictures of any paperwork Henry had left lying around. When Henry noted the paperwork on his desk, he frowned in disbelief at his carelessness. On one corner of a loose sheaf were the coordinates for his test site. Henry groaned out loud.

"Someone knows about my laser drill, the test site and goodness knows what else. They may have accessed my safe at some point. I seem to recall mislaying some papers of mine a year ago. They weren't at all complete so it didn't bother me at the..."

"I don't suppose those papers had some early calculations and formulas on them?" prompted Rizzo.

When Henry nodded his shoulders dropped. As impossible as it seemed only moments ago, it now looked likely that someone had broken into his lab the previous year and absconded with those early scribblings. They knew about his test site, they knew about his prototype and the actual device. They may have perceived his early calculations as being more advanced than they were. If they used those to configure a pirated replica...?

"I'm not saying that I believe *everything*, but I'm coming around to the possibility that my designs may have been duplicated by persons unknown, possibly inferior designs based on those early doodles. That would account for the fact that the flawed designs were studied by you from a memory stick that survived the underwater event. That also means those persons are manufacturing the device right now."

TWELVE

Henry and Rizzo talked well into the afternoon and evening after placing his papers back in the safe downstairs. They discussed a wide variety of subjects, possibilities, theories and relationships. Henry accepted that he was no longer speaking directly to a young, former student. Her demeanour and language constituted an entirely different personality. While the sudden change was a little overwhelming and often confusing, it was welcomed by Henry who felt more comfortable dealing with his student on a more equal footing in both maturity and intelligence, than before.

Rizzo showed a remarkable understanding of his concepts in drill design and practical theory on locations suitable for exploration and experimentation. He had asked at one point if he should discontinue referring to her as Rizzo. That was answered in the negative when he was reminded that the younger Rachelle still resided in her mind, albeit sulkily quiet.

Some 'intellect' you are. Can't tell the difference between utter sadness and sulking!

Rizzo ignored the remark or revelation, whatever it was. There were more important fish to fry than worrying about Rache's hurt feelings. The papers she studied regarding Henry's designs came as a shock to her. It was also shameful that she had spent many years accepting his flawed designs as being responsible for the end of the world as it was known. Recollections of Henry's obsessive need to record everything in hard copy surfaced as Rizzo reflected on her past associations with him. It stood to reason that he wouldn't entrust his most precious ideas to technology, especially when that technology had previously wiped out months of his hard work when a faculty laptop's lithium battery exploded one night setting fire to half the campus.

Something of a dire nature had befallen the doctor's research. Whoever was responsible for the surveillance devices they'd uncovered had access to inferior designs. Using those flawed designs to beat Henry to the prize, to obtain almost limitless energy from beneath the earth. Henry did not bring about that end. His slandered image and almost demonised reputation were ill-founded and Rizzo was as guilty as the rest of humanity in pointing that finger.

"I am so very, very sorry, Henry."

"Whatever for?" he asked suddenly broken from his reveries.

"I was just as quick to blame you as everyone else. I grasped hold of the fact that your math was less than reliable during our classes and immediately surmised that you had erred in your designs. I do remember now that you always, without fail, had someone check over your figures before presenting them in your papers or journals."

"Was it, though?"

"Was what?"

"The formula flawed."

"Um, had to be, right? Overshot the mark and..."

"Pierced the core?"

"What are you saying?"

"You're assuming that someone was too stupid to see the flaw in the formula. Fairly basic stuff for boffins like us, wouldn't you say? I get that the math is beyond the layman..."

"Yeah, I see what you mean. I figured it out and I'm no genius."

"I wouldn't go so far as to say that. You have to have a mind for our speciality to understand the methodology for acquiring the density figures then applying the formulas. We know the mass and the volume of the earth thanks to Henry Cavendish's formula. We simply place those known quantities into the equation $p = m/V$. Anyone in our sphere can arrive at the same answers. Configuring my laser drill to the correct intensity levels and cut-outs is elementary computer code. Nothing extraordinary in any of it. I've simply used exiting elements and common information in a different configuration to come up with a basic design. Much like poor old Robert Kearns."

"Who?"

"A relatively unknown inventor who came up with the earliest version of intermittent windscreen wipers back in the 20th century. He arranged a set of readily-available electronic components in a particular manner that allowed what he called, the blinking eye wiper, to come about. After a protracted legal battle that saw him lose almost everything including his family, he finally won the right to his patent and the accordant royalties he was due from Ford and other car manufacturers using his design."

"I don't think anyone is disputing your name on the design. I think most people wanted to disassociate themselves with any part of it."

"That isn't my point."

"What then?"

"What if it wasn't a mistake?"

"Why would someone deliberately... Oh, the Eldorado theory?"

"Maybe."

It had been postulated for aeons that the earth's core was made of the heaviest metals sinking to the centre. Namely; gold. Tons and tons of pure gold swirling away in the centre of the earth along with other minerals creating our magnetic field to defend the planet against the cosmos.

"You can't possibly think someone would deliberately try to tap into the core in the hopes of getting rich? Especially when anyone in the know accepts that the core is predominantly made up of an iron-nickel alloy. That's just..."

"Greed. Known to subvert the natures of humankind forever."

"You said yourself that it must have been someone with an intimate knowledge of our fields of expertise. If that was true, they would also know that it was pure conjecture about the mineral makeup of the core, and that attempting to rupture it was hazardous in the extreme, if it were possible."

"My device made that possible...in the end. If what you say is true."

Henry began to feel the immense pressure of responsibility begin to burden his already taxed mind and body. Events that had yet to transpire, indicating an end to all life on earth, were suddenly thrust upon the hapless doctor. The enormity of the possible outcomes derived from the misuse of the device Henry had conceived, threatened to cripple his thought processes. It was too much to take in at once.

The sudden slump in the doctor's shoulders along with his stricken face, made Rizzo wince with sympathy. It wasn't difficult to imagine what her old mentor was feeling. He was a good and kind man, as evidenced by his nature in sitting a lonely vigil by her hospital bedside for nearly a year, expecting, but receiving, little reward. He didn't deserve the treatment dished out to him by the world and he certainly didn't deserve to shoulder the responsibility for someone else's actions with his stolen plans.

"Time for you to put on your other cap, Henry. The sci-fi nerd's cap. I know how much you love old sci-fi movies and theories. Almost as much as I do. Can it be changed?"

"The past?" he asked dejectedly.

"My past, not yours. Yours hasn't happened yet. Not for another five years."

"Oh boy. I'm a scientist first, a pragmatist. I dwell in known facts and provable theorems. I don't dabble in fantasy, Rachelle...er...Rizzo."

"I'm living proof that time travel is possible. Not in the whole 'flux capacitor, flying DeLorean' way, but with 'shooting a data package through an Einstein-Rosen bridge' kind of way. I'm from the future, Henry. Time to put your big boy pants on and accept that...or not. Make up your mind whether you believe me and start being part of a solution. Otherwise, I'll leave and find some way to end this on my own."

"It isn't that simple..."

"Too fucking bad, mate! We don't have time for a whole lot of hand-holding trepidation here. Either you accept or you don't. I don't give a fuck one way or the other. I'd prefer to work with you on solutions but I'll walk away quickly if you continue to feel sorry for yourself over something that hasn't happened yet."

"Who are you?" Henry asked suddenly.

"Rachelle Rizzoli, banged up, stuffed up, Rachelle-bloody Rizzoli. I went through too much shit with one bastard of a man to take any crap from another. Now grow the fuck up, Henry or take a hike!" Rizzo exclaimed.

The outburst left both of them breathless. It had the intended effect on Henry, to make him escape the bubble of internalisations he was heading into. For Rizzo, she regretted immediately the force with which she unloaded on her old mentor. It had to have been mind-bendingly difficult for him to come to terms with all the information thrust upon him in a short time.

Say you're sorry.

"No, I won't."

"No, you won't what?" asked Henry looking very confused.

"Rache is demanding that I apologise. I refused. I won't say sorry to a man again...ever."

"That chap did some kind of number on you, didn't he?"

"You have no idea."

"Yet, during your narrative earlier you intimated that you might try to recreate those children with him?"

"I have a veritable arsenal of defence moves against any male thinking they can take advantage of me now. The mothering instinct is very strong in me despite my having no recall of my children's faces. I have to try."

"Why not try with someone else in that case?"

"You offering?"

"What? No...I..."

"Oh, don't go to pieces on me. I was kidding. I know my children came from my union with that monster, Robert Rizzoli. No other combination will produce the same results."

"No other combination or unions with *anyone* will produce the same results. You must know that?"

"I know," said Rizzo sighing.

"Wishing it won't make it so."

"I know."

"Yet, you're still going to try?"

"I know it doesn't make any sense to you. It doesn't make that much sense to me either. I just have this inescapable urge in me to make it happen, to recapture what I've lost. It is the single most important thing to me at the moment. Even more pressing than stopping the end of the world, if you can believe that."

Henry nodded his understanding, "There's precious little you can do at the moment anyway. I can do a bit of digging and snooping while you're attending to...other things for the time being? We do have five years."

"I have a lot less than that to achieve my purpose. It may be too late already...wait, no, it isn't. I didn't fall pregnant immediately."

"You say you fell pregnant? Not planned, then?"

"No, not planned. We both felt the same way at the time, though, so it was natural for us to get married.

Rizzo, I'm scared.

"Suck it up, girl..."

"Rachelle!" Henry exclaimed. "Sorry, Rizzo. I assume you were talking to Rachelle Shaw just then?" Rizzo nodded uncertainly.

"Well, you have in there a young, vibrant young woman whom I had the pleasure of teaching not so long ago. A vulnerable, intelligent and attractive young lady. You haven't told me exactly what happened to you but I understand you were crippled?"

Another nod from Rizzo with a confused expression.

"Don't you see? You have been given something very, very rare and extraordinary if everything you say is true. You have been allowed to start afresh in a young, healthy body at the prime of your life. What you fail to realise is that you were not only physically crippled by your experiences. You were turned into a twisted and bitter woman by the sound of it. You are continuing to be that woman. Your essence, your core, if you will, has been corrupted and you aren't embracing the fantastic miracle afforded you. You are without a shred of compassion for even yourself. Inside you is the young person you used to be and should become once more. She needs you. And you need her even more."

Rizzo stared at her old mentor, so removed in age from the man attending her in the hospital. A far younger man stood before her and she saw the gleam in his eyes that she once observed during her classes with him. She finally saw the love there which she refused to acknowledge or ignored in her younger years. How different life might have been had she allowed his affections to come to fruition. She could have done a lot worse. She had done a lot worse!

Damn right she was bitter after her experiences! She had every right to be. Didn't she? Introspection was never a strong point with her and even less so after the accident. Crippled mind? How dare he? Yet, even as she questioned it, she recognised the validity of the statement. Her life was one of survival, of subsistence after hospital. From the brink of total despair where life meant nothing, to one of survival for the sake of her children.

She assumed that was so without having any direct recollections of it. Her children. Try as she might, she was unable to conjure up any pictures of them, only emotions surrounding them. It was quite surreal. Like staring at a blank computer screen. She saw nothing yet felt every last emotion connected to Gabs and Lorenzo. Her behaviour must have affected them as well. It would not have been possible to keep that twisted personality hidden from them. There were too many years where Rizzo had felt hollow and horrible, which was projected outward without her ever fully realising it, or caring. Her mind mirrored her horrific body in every detail. The pain and suffering she endured manifested themselves into a verbal avalanche of hostility toward everyone.

Henry was right. She was still a cripple. The truth stunned her.

"Sorry, Rizzo. I can see that I hurt you. You must understand though, the young person I fell in love with no longer exists in the person I see before me. You must not waste the opportunity to build something better in the short time you have left if we fail to halt the cataclysm. I think I have a plan regarding that. You must see to building some bridges for yourself."

"You need my help," she offered weakly.

"Not in your present state, I don't. You aren't any help to anyone, let alone yourself while you continue to allow your brutalised personality to reign. Go find yourself again. Look hard at the mirror, talk to that inner you. Allow her to guide you on your new journey to completeness. I can't say forget about your children, even though you have done so, literally. All I can say is that you mustn't be ruled by those emotions you carry concerning the children. There is you to consider and you are important. Important enough to matter to me and the woman residing in you, in need of some compassion and understanding. She may not be around much longer according to your experiences so far."

Rizzo couldn't be certain but it seemed a tear may have formed in the corner of Henry's eye before he abruptly turned away.

"Henry? What do you hope to do?"

"You say we have five years before the cataclysm takes place, right?"

Rizzo nods.

"And that I am working for a private corporation manning a drilling platform at the bottom of the Bougainville Trench when it happens?"

Another nod.

"In that case, it won't be too difficult to change the course of history. Or in my case, the future. I simply won't be there or with the private firm."

THIRTEEN

The air was pounding, the lights swirling and pulsating in time to the electric music blasting from the speakers beside the stage. The heavy-metal techno-pop mix coming from the relatively unheard-of band whipped the excited teenagers into a frenzy of frenetic movement and rhythm.

Caught up in the chaotic environment of sweaty, near-naked bodies contorting to the sound was Rizzo, revelling in the atmosphere. The complicated riffs ripped through the audience while Robert Rizzoli shredded his guitar, seemingly lost to the world around him, unaware of the adulation from the young females and males in the crowd screaming their encouragement. The guitar solo was extended far beyond the rehearsed arrangement, with the rest of the band sucked into the fevered improvisation. It was like they were back in their garage simply jamming like crazy and enjoying the hell out of it.

Techno Jam is what they labelled their music, a new kind of funky heavy metal with a whole lot of everything else thrown in. Almost like electric jazz in the way that it became a hodgepodge of styles, instruments and different personalities lighting up randomly for solo performances throughout the pieces. The crowd ate up the original compositions thumping their eardrums and pounding their senses into a mesmerising euphoria.

Rizzo saw only the front man, Robert Rizzoli, in the posture of a rock God, eating up the chords and punishing his instrument like there was no tomorrow. She had forgotten completely how charismatic the man was when he was in his element. It was the 'low-key', almost impromptu concert that eventually launched him and his band into the stratosphere. Rachelle Shaw had attended the concert that night all those years ago, falling head over heels for the young demi-god as she danced and jumped and screamed with all the others.

Robert and his band were signed by a major label the following morning, after previous talks with executives. The fifty-million-dollar deal for five albums over five years would see the band become the top-selling Australian band of the 22nd century. When Robert finally looked up from his guitar, he noticed Rizzo in the crowd near the front of the stage for the first time. He beamed his pearly whites at her before disappearing into the music once more.

The roadie that grabbed her sleeve at the end of the concert almost ended up on the floor with a broken arm before Rizzo realised he was merely holding out a backstage pass for her. She picked him up easily from the dance floor with an apologetic smile. The roadie grimaced and massaged his arm before storming off with a scowl.

It wasn't until several hours later that Rizzo finally had some time alone with Robert, walking from the reception hall where the party was held along the deserted streets of the inner city. They were headed in the general direction of Central Station to catch a train to Milton. They had an hour to wait at the station for the next train.

"That was off the charts fantastic, you know that, right?"

"Pays the bills," said Robert with a shrug.

"You can't fool me. I saw you up there. You were into it in a big way," Rizzo argued.

"Oh, sure. I get lost in the music just as much as anyone else, but it's only a means to an end."

They came to a bench where they sat to wait for the train. The platform had only a handful of other commuters in various states of inebriation or simply passed out.

"What's that mean?"

"I mean I can use the money I get from doing that to pursue my true passion."

"Which is?"

"I already told you. In the library?"

"I never even heard you play anything like that," Rizzo blurted out before she could stop herself.

"Of course, you haven't," he said with a look of concern. "How could you have?"

"Right. I meant I couldn't picture you playing anything like that."

"I had to be dragged kicking and screaming to play in that band by those guys. I couldn't believe they bothered asking me."

"How did it come about?" Rizzo asked, knowing the story.

"They heard me playing an acoustic gig in a coffee shop one

day as they walked past and invited me to jam with them in their garage studio the following day. We just sort of clicked; I suppose. I had superior music skills to them in some areas like composition and arrangements, while they had the grunge that I lacked at first. I wasn't really into any other music than classical. Guitar and piano mainly. Bit of violin and cello as well if I feel like it."

"Get real! Violin and cello? No fucking way!" she said punching him lightly on the arm.

"What?"

"You can't be serious?"

"As a death in the family," said Robert with a frown.

"Sorry?"

"Serious as a death in the family?" he explained patiently.

"Oh. I never... I mean, I wouldn't have believed it possible given what I saw tonight," admitted Rizzo.

"Last night," he corrected. "Are you coming home with me?"

"You sure you want me to?"

Are you sure you want to?

Rizzo hadn't heard from Rache for a time, expecting her to be still sulking about the decision to pursue a relationship with her former husband. They'd argued about it...vehemently. With the threat of Rache conjuring up weird and vile acts in her head to put off any kind of intimacy occurring, Rizzo began to ignore her completely.

"Yeah, I want you to. A perfect way to cap off a perfect night...er...morning."

"Inviting me in for a nightcap, then?"

"Ah, out of luck there, I'm afraid."

"What, nothing at all? Not even a cold, wet one?"

"If you're referring to cold, wet soda water or orange juice, yes. If you're referring to anything stronger? Forget it. I don't drink, as much as you think I have or should."

"Bit of weed?"

"Uh-uh. No weed, no pills, no junk, no nothing. My body is a temple which I hope to keep pure and functional for a long time yet. I get off on music, that's my euphoria. Classical music. Mozart, Beethoven, Bach, Rachmaninov, all of them. I live, breathe and eat classical music. Unless I'm doing a gig of that other stuff to pay for the rent and build up my bank account for when I enrol in the

Academy."

"You'll have one helluva bank account by the end of the day."

"What do you mean?"

"Oh, a little birdie tells me that record deal will be formerly offered to you tomorrow. I saw the label execs sitting in the back row tables for an hour taking copious notes and looking way out of place at your concert."

"Gig. It was just a small gig. Hardly a concert."

"You had them in the palm of your hand. The audience and the execs. They saw the effect you were having on the crowd. They know a meal ticket when they see it. That was some of your best playing in there..."

"There you go again. How would you know that? Are you a secret groupie?"

"Yeah, you got me. I've seen you play before, "Rizzo blabbed out as she tried to hide her embarrassment at being caught out lying again.

You're going to get yourself in a right pickle at this rate. Pathetic at lying and worse at seduction, you are.

Robert eyed her warily, wondering just what it was with this strange woman. She was hot, he gave her that. She had to be smart to be a doctor, albeit a research doctor. Why he had a lower opinion of one over the other he couldn't be sure. When he spied her in the audience his heart leapt in his chest. He wasn't sure why about that either. He didn't have room in his life for an entanglement. And Rachelle Shaw seemed like the worst kind of entanglement in his mind.

Robert wasn't one for one-night stands or casual flings. In truth, he'd only been intimate with two other females in his life, one being a clumsy high school affair and the other, many years later. Although he stayed with that later person for nearly a year, she became far too clingy and suffocating for him to continue the relationship.

From the time Robert received his first toy piano, on which he became an overnight virtuoso...in his mind, he found a passion that would drive his ambitions well into his adult life. A genuine, cheap, upright piano entered his world as a six-year-old when his parents recognised their child's great enthusiasm and drive after the toy piano was destroyed through overuse. With the piano came lessons which Robert consumed like it was his last meal. He outgrew one piano tutor after another, each one proclaiming their student to be a prodigy brought about by their careful ministrations.

Robert had a full library of classical music scores and recordings by his fifteenth birthday when he was presented with a baby grand piano costing his parents a small fortune. He'd worn out the upright and was using an electric keyboard for his lessons until he told his parents it wasn't good enough to get him where he needed to be. He required the tonality and texture of a decent piano to understand the nuances of the scores he studied in great depth.

Sending his parents into near penury, Robert somehow managed to keep up his lessons to gain the satisfaction of his more experienced tutors, costing the family more and more money.

By his eighteenth year, his parents could no longer afford the burden. They were bankrupt and penniless. Robert's father's business had collapsed due to the economic hard times of the period when the globe was suffering another financial crisis with stock markets crumbling and tower-divers a common story. Robert was forced to consider alternatives to his life-long dream. The hope of entering the Adelaide Academy of Music drifted farther and farther from his grasp. Until the band came his way.

As much as he loathed sinking to the depths of rock music, he could see no other way to support himself until he could save his tuition fees. Scholarships were impossible to get due to the financial crisis. Short of becoming a thief, he saw no other way. It wasn't like he was a gifted student in any other capacity. Working some deadbeat job was out. Not because of its nature and drudgery, but because he would never be suitably qualified, experienced or motivated enough to be hired. Robert Rizzoli wasn't dumb by any means, just not wired that way. Music was his life.

The money the label execs were tossing around the previous day still boggled his mind. He and his band members were still trying to grasp the enormity of it before their gig last night. The other band members saw the execs at the rear of the small venue and they felt the small crowd erupting with their original tunes. Then they gasped in awe as their lead guitarist and singer began shredding his guitar with an impromptu solo that set the crowd on fire. The atmosphere was electric...literally. Pyrotechnics and electric mayhem effects were part and parcel of the show, thanks to their tech-savvy crew and management team.

Though some money terms had been tossed around casually in the order of millions, no one had placed a firm offer on the table to date. Everyone involved with the band saw that changing immediately following the gig. It was all anyone spoke of during the after-party. They could all use the dough that was for sure, none more so than Robert who wished desperately to repay his parents and get them out of the shit. One of the execs approached him after the gig to set up an appointment for him and his band manager the following day...today.

So, Rachelle Shaw, hot as she was and smart as she seemed, was an entanglement he couldn't afford. He regretted bringing her home, regretted befriending her and regretted most of all; falling in love with her. He knew it the moment he saw her. Then the commotion separated them.

Shit, he thought for the umpteenth time, while cosying up to her on the threadbare settee in the cramped living room, which doubled up as his bedroom. The train had picked them up without them realising it; taken them to Milton where they walked in a daze to Robert's small apartment.

Before either of them understood where the time had gone, they woke in each other's arms after a sweaty, lust-fuelled orgy of pure, untainted sex.

Slut!

FOURTEEN

It was a whirlwind few weeks following their initial night of delicious debauchery. While Robert was attempting to be as aloof and restrained as possible in his affections, Rizzo was revelling in the newfound physicality. The two bodies melded together seamlessly when they found time to be with one another, a rareness, with Robert's band, *Electric Ego*, getting signed up by the record label for an obscene amount of money in their view and headed straight into extended rehearsals for a tour and a studio album.

Finding herself in a bit of a quandary regarding her newfound passion and excited libido, Rizzo walked along the path winding through a local park on Barroona Road near Robert's apartment in Milton.

Well, well, well.

"Three holes in the ground?"

Ha, ha! I wouldn't give up your day job just yet...oh wait, you did.

"You know there's no point in me taking the job now."

No? How about if old Dr Thoms succeeds?

"All the more reason."

What are you going to do for your...well...lifetime if he does? Screw yourself into oblivion until you can't open your legs anymore. Just going to breed more and more brats into the world? There was an old lady who lived in a shoe. She had so many kids her cunt fell out!

"That is really vulgar, even for you. Kind of funny, though."

WAKE UP RIZZO!!!

"Don't have a cow."

God, you're sounding more like me every day.

"I am you! Remember?"

"You are a crabby old cripple, not a young woman talking like she's fresh out of her teens."

"I'm not a cripple anymore," Rizzo said with relish.

No, you're just a slut now.

"Listen to Miss Puritanical. Anyone'd think you were a virgin before I took over. Only I know it isn't true."

I get it, you're in lust. Okay, get over it, move on with your life.

"You don't get it, do you? My children were my life. I'm doing everything in my power to replicate that."

You said yourself that it wasn't possible to replicate your children.

"Replicate having children, not *my* children. My body remembers and my brain retains the emotions around them."

Bullshit! You're in my body and it doesn't remember what hasn't happened yet. You're projecting your fantasies with the hope they'll stick. What the fuck happened to you? I thought you said you were mature and intelligent? You're acting like some love-struck moron.

"Is that really so bad? After all that I've been through, don't I deserve a bit of happiness?"

And then everything comes crashing down again when he starts using my body for batting practice. How far along is that, by the way?

"It's not the same as it was. He's...different. Very different from the man I knew. He doesn't drink, doesn't do drugs and keeps himself healthy and fit! The bozo I knew never touched an exercise bike or a treadmill."

You told me that he changes once he goes on tour. That starts in a week.

"I didn't take all those self-defence classes for nothing, Rache. If he starts any of that shit with me, he's in for a big surprise. Until then, he hasn't done a thing to make me feel anything but treasured and wanted."

Treasured and wanted? Listen to yourself, would you? You're pathetic. Vomit in the mouth stuff.

"Hey, you. Whatcha up to?" said Robert almost out of breath from his jog around the neighbourhood.

"Hi, Robert. Didn't know you ran this way?"

"I don't normally. I don't have any set routines if that's what you're thinking. I like to...whew! I like to explore a bit, you know? See parts of the neighbourhood I haven't seen yet or been for a while."

"Want to sit and catch your breath?"

"Yeah, that'd be great. I have something I wanted to discuss with you anyway. You left the apartment before I got the chance."

Robert fairly collapsed to the soft, freshly-mown grass, while Rizzo chose a gentler descent. They sat quietly for a few moments while Robert concentrated on his breathing. He usually ran for at least an hour every second day, keeping his muscled physique lithe and trim. Not for the first time did Rizzo feel the animal magnetism drawing her to him. She would have loved nothing more than to rip his clothes off at that very moment and make passionate love to him right there on the grass for all the world to see.

Slut!

"Listen, lovely lady. We haven't known each other all that long but I get the feeling you might like me as much as I like...love...you. I think it will be a big crimp in my plans but I wonder if you'd do me the honour of marrying me?" he asked, barely whispering the last words.

Shit!

"Wow! That was kind of sudden. Are you sure about that?"

"Never been surer of anything in my life. I think I fell for you the first moment I saw you. I felt like I'd been hit by lightning. I love you Rachelle Shaw and would like to know if you'd care to become Rachelle Rizzoli...unless you want to keep your maiden name, that is? All's fair in this modern world, huh?"

"You say it will put a huge crimp in your plans?"

"Nothing we can't work around, I'm sure. Well? Don't keep me hanging here. Sort of a bit vulnerable right now."

"Oh, don't go getting all sooky now. Of course I'll marry you..."

Fuck!

"But there's something you have to know first."

What? Wait, no! You can't tell him the truth!

"Wouldn't matter about anything in your past if that's what you're about to reveal. I love you for who you are right now and nothing is going to change that. I've never felt this way before about anyone. I struggle to make sense of things when you aren't around me. You make me..."

"You need to stop now before you get any more cliché. I'm not about to reveal skeletons from my closet...yet. I may have a few little confessions for you later on, but not now. No, I have something about the present to talk to you about and it's important. Before I accept your proposal, you have to know."

Oh boy!

"I'm pregnant," Rizzo stated loudly and proudly with a smile that resonated with her profound happiness.

"I see. Who's the proud father, then?" asked Robert with a face that dropped a thousand miles, the shutters coming down on the windows to his soul.

"You, of course, don't be silly," said Rachelle with a minute inkling of foreboding.

"You told me you were taking precautions," he said in a flat tone.

"I was. I mean, I am. I mean, I missed taking one, that's all."

"I see."

"Is that all you have to say?"

"It's a big announcement and a lot to take in right now," he said with a voice devoid of all emotion.

"Aren't you happy?"

"About having a child? No."

"Why not?"

"Didn't factor a child in. Couldn't. It doesn't fit in with my plans. We'll have to make the arrangements."

"What arrangements?"

"To get rid of it, of course. I..."

"Are you insane? I'm not having an abortion!"

"Really? What do you intend to do then?"

"Become a mother, naturally."

"Aren't you forgetting one small fact?"

"What fact?"

"The Pop Bureau?"

Robert was referring to the Bureau for Population Feasibility and Adjustment. A very wordy euphemism for the department of birth control. Strict protocols were to be followed during the 22nd century in a world that was heavily over-populated. Restrictions on conception and birth affected 99% of the globe. An application had to be made well in advance of conception. Applying after the fact was almost always rejected unless there were extending circumstances well beyond the control of either parent. Very few exceptions were ever made with those kinds of limitations imposed.

Fuck!

"Damn! I'd forgotten about that. Still, if we sign the application and state that I was taking a defective form of contraception?"

"Why would I do that? I don't want a child, Rachelle. I have plans and they don't allow for a child in my life right now. I don't want to get involved with all the red tape either. Much easier to abort now and reconsider later when we can plan it properly and fill out the applications as per the law?"

"I won't abort. I'm pregnant with twins."

"Oh, well, that's even worse. In the unlikely event that you're granted an exception, they *will* terminate one of the pair, as you know. They will never allow two!"

He's right and you should have known.

Robert was growing redder in the face and angrier the longer the argument continued. Rizzo saw the warning signs clearly, remembering the trigger points from the past.

"You have enough money to take care of us and our children, Robert."

"That isn't the point. First of all, I don't want children right now. If I did, I certainly wouldn't want two at once, even with permission. Secondly, you won't get permission from the Pop Bureau *after* you've conceived. It's practically a term of imprisonment these days. They're really cracking down on it. As far as the money is concerned, it's none of your business just yet what money I have or don't have."

"Of course, it is. We're living as a de-facto couple, Robert. I moved in with you, remember? That is as good as being husband and wife in the eyes of the law."

Robert raised his right hand suddenly which made Rizzo react with an instinctual movement. She grasped the raised hand with both of hers, bending his wrist back painfully to a near breaking point behind his back.

"Don't you dare even think about striking me, *mate*," Rizzo rasped between clenched teeth.

"Let me go. I was only going to knock the stick insect off your head. What the fuck is wrong with you?"

"You what?"

"One of those ugly stick things flew onto your head. I was just going to..."

Rizzo let go of his hand while she screamed in alarm, brushing her head wildly with flaying hands. Managing to squash the insect into her hair made her feel a thousand times worse. The morning sickness came upon her in an instant, causing her to heave convulsively to the side.

Robert waited impatiently to one side of the heaving woman with a determined scowl on his face, repulsed by the smell, the situation and most of all, the woman he had stupidly and mistakenly proposed to. He felt a great sigh of relief welling up in him despite his feelings toward Rachelle Shaw. He was immensely grateful to see her true colours before he made the monumental error of marrying her.

"I withdraw my proposal and I want nothing to do with you or your child...children."

"*Our* children," Rizzo spat with venom.

"Nope. Not even close. I can't have children thanks to a bike accident a few years back. Gave myself a vasectomy with a wheel spoke that severed the vas deferens. Doctors said they might be able to repair it at some point if I felt strongly enough to want it done and could afford it."

"Bullshit! They were wrong. I've seen the fluid come out of you."

"Yep, you did. That's part of a voluntary vasectomy as well. There's still an experience of ejaculation and all the joy associated with that, but no live wrigglers. Proven with several samples I've had to provide since then," Robert explained with the pain of unrequited love etched on his features. "I might have forgiven you the fact that you've been sleeping around behind my back. I might have been persuaded to fill out an application with the Pop Bureau to keep the child. I might even have forgiven you for what you just did to me when all I tried to do was wipe away an insect. I can't forgive *all* of those things.

"As much as I love you...loved you, I won't forgive you. I would have been forced to commit to a family by my honour and sense of responsibility if I was truly the father. Knowing the children aren't mine means you aren't worth giving up my life for. Having children would see my dream of attending the Academy turn to dust. I want you out of my apartment by the time I return tomorrow morning."

"You're wrong. I haven't been with anyone else. They're your children," Rizzo insisted.

Robert gave her an oily smile of smug satisfaction, "Know

when I gave my last sample, Rachelle? Two days ago. Armed with the knowledge that I was going to propose to you, I made an appointment to discuss a reversal procedure with my doctor in case you and I might want children at a later date. He wasn't optimistic about the outcomes and he confirmed yesterday that my sample contained no live sperm. I have the letter from my physician to prove it any time you care to see it, or think you can try for a paternity suit. You won't get one cent of my money, no matter how much of it I have. Get out of my life and stay out!"

Robert stormed off leaving Rizzo with a sinking feeling. Her knees gradually gave way, allowing her to sink slowly to the grass. Absently brushing at the fresh grass stains on her knee, Rizzo reflected on the dramatic turn of events. It was impossible! She'd had children with Robert in the past. It didn't make any sense.

Didn't you ever get a paternity test done?

"Of course not. Why would I? I never slept with a man around the time I met Robert. And I had the two kids a year apart, married to Robert at the time. He has to be mistaken or...lying."

I've heard of a case where a woman had sex with a man only once and fell pregnant twice. Apparently, the sperm fertilised both eggs but only produced two single embryos a year apart. Kangaroos do something like that with a system called embryonic diapause, but I think they have to have sex twice to accomplish it.

"Fascinating! Only, it doesn't explain how I managed to get pregnant by another man when you know as well as I do that I haven't been near any other men. Care to explain that?"

That you know of.

"What's that horseshit supposed to mean?"

Not sure. I get the sense of some missing time somewhere.

"Between when and when?"

Think of it another way. Who is the only other man that you've been in contact with?

"I...what? You're confusing me."

Think about it, Rizzo. If it wasn't Robert then who is the only other man you've been with in the last few weeks?

"No one!"

Not true. You stayed overnight at a man's house, didn't you?

"Henry? Do you mean Dr Henry Thoms? Yeah, technically, we stayed there but nothing happened. You know that."

Do I?

"Now, you're totally confusing me. Henry put us up in his spare bedroom while he went downstairs into his lab. I even locked the door before I went to sleep."

An interior privacy latch can be opened from the other side of the door with a screwdriver for safety reasons.

"This is ridiculous. Nothing happened. Pretty sure I would have woken up if a man had snuck into my room and proceeded to have his way with me. I may have only had full possession of your body for a short time but no way is that going to happen without me knowing."

All I'm saying is, I think I've lost some time there.

"He wouldn't do something like..."

He's besotted by us...me. He has it so bad that he gave up his lifelong dream of being a professor. Who knows what a man like that is capable of? What was in that last drink he mixed for you before you went to bed? Timing's about right for a pregnancy of your term, isn't it?

"Are you suggesting I was drugged and raped? By a college professor?"

Not sure what I'm saying just yet. I'm trying logic in a very illogical scenario. Robert Rizzoli is incapable of having children according to him and his doctor. He has a letter to prove it he says. By process of elimination, it leaves only one other possibility.

"But Henry..."

Is a man. A man with strong feelings towards you. Strong enough to sit vigil by your bedside for nearly a year. Bringing us around to another very disturbing piece of the puzzle. If Robert was unable to produce children, when he married you, he entered into that marriage knowing that. You coerced him into marriage by falling pregnant when he had no desire for children in his immediate future. He was more or less forced to continue with the band to provide for his family while giving up on his ultimate hopes and dreams, his classical interests, the academy?

"What are you saying?"

Think about it. Smashing his dreams with pregnancy by another man? Regardless of whether you knew who the father was or wasn't, it still wrecked his life.

"You saying I drove him to drink?"

Rachelle didn't have to answer her question for Rizzo to know the truth of it. The enormity of the revelation caused Rizzo to sway slightly. It was a disturbing piece of information if it was true. It changed her previous perceptions entirely, shattered her past existence. The fractured pictures eked their way through to her as Rizzo saw more and more of her previous life unfold in a new light. Armed with the new insights many odd comments and arguments became understandable and plausible in her mind.

Through no fault of her own, Rizzo had demolished a young man's dreams and insulted his love by becoming pregnant with another man's child. The sea of nausea threatened to see her collapse. Only her strong will prevented it. It was a huge slice of reality to take on board, knowing what a lie her past life had been built upon. At least, for her. In Robert Rizzoli's eyes, he was married to a woman of loose morals and a liar. He would have known all along that the children weren't his. The second one, Lorenzo, would have been the final icing on the cake for him, sending him over the edge into an abyss of self-loathing, resentment and suffering.

Could it have happened the way Rachelle pointed out? Could a bizarre anomaly have taken place in her body whereby two of her eggs were fertilised at once but only descended to the uterus a year apart? Stranger things have happened, she supposed. The human body was still a great mystery withholding many secrets and fascinating exceptions.

While Rizzo tossed around all the possibilities in her head, one emotion began to take root deep within her; anger. A wave of anger that stemmed from a very independent female knowing she had been violated. Without her permission, without her consent, without her knowledge. Henry Thoms! In an instant, he changed from a beloved mentor in Rizzo's eyes to one of a sadistic pervert. A rapist! It had to be true. There was no other possible explanation. Henry was the only other man she'd been in contact with during the elapsed time when conception could have occurred. It caused the young woman to tremble with impotent rage. Impotent because she had no one nearby on whom to vent.

Well, aren't you a nasty piece of work? All this time playing the aggrieved victim when it was you causing a young man's grief and anguish. Coming over all pious to me. You broke his heart just then and did a lot worse when you married him the first time.

"I...it...shit!"

*Yeah, shit is right. You're pregnant with twins in a world that won't allow even one child without the appropriate forms being filled out in triplicate **before** conception. Any idea what you're going to do now?*

"Besides confronting a malevolent pervert, you mean?"

You have bigger fish to fry than attempting to besmirch the name of a respected former professor and geophysicist. If he did accept that position with the Department of Energy, you have no way of gaining access to him now without giving yourself away to the assassin. Do we even trust him enough to believe he'll do what he says?

"What do you mean?"

You say you were sent back in time to prevent Armageddon. Thoms is a slime ball, a sleaze-bucket with hidden agendas and I wouldn't trust him as far as I could throw him. Maybe he did what he did because you insulted his intelligence when you believed that his design was flawed. Maybe he took it as a huge blow to his delicate ego even though you agreed that his design wasn't flawed after viewing his files. Maybe he was just always a sleaze-bag with a penchant for young women and you presented the perfect opportunity for him to carry out his twisted fantasies.

"You think he'll do nothing about the possibility that someone screwed with his design?"

What if you handed him the knowledge to make his design work exactly the way it happened? What if he intends to deliberately puncture the core now?

"That doesn't make any sense. Why would he..."

Twisted minds do twisted things. He now has the method of being the first person to drill down to the core of the planet. Name in lights. Big-time scientist. First to accomplish an impossible task. He would be heralded alongside greats like Sir Edmund Hilary and Scott of the Antarctic.

"No, no, no. He's an eminent..."

He's a scum bag male with an ego the size of a house. He drugged and raped you.

"We don't know that for certain."

Yes, we do. Face it, it's true. You know what we have to do now.

"I do?"

Absolutely. We have to get onto the Bougainville Belle *once he's deployed there.*

"Oh, you're funny."

I wasn't joking. When he starts that shit on the bottom of the ocean floor, we have to be there to stop him.

"I can't believe I'm hearing this. How the fuck do we get onto a deep-sea drilling platform that only one or two submersibles in the world can reach? Even if we did find a way down there, what could we do? Sabotage it?"

When silence greeted Rizzo, she understood it was precisely what Rachelle meant.

"No. You're wrong. My priority is to make sure my babies are born safely. Nothing is more important than that for us both. The whole end of the world thing doesn't happen for a while..."

Are you sure about that? Haven't you already noticed differences occurring? What's to say that history will repeat itself in the exact order or with the same timing? You're fucking with the natural order, mate? And you better be damn sure you get this right. I don't know how much longer I'm going to be around, but my body sure as heck will be and my...our legacy. We need to make sure they have a world in which to grow. Life underground in some steel city doesn't sound like a very appealing place to raise children.

"It wasn't. However, to have a place for children to live, we must first ensure those children are granted entry into the world. If the Pop Bureau find out about me and the twins, it'll be immediate abortion and a stretch behind bars. How could I have forgotten about that? How did I get around it the first time around? Oh, wait. He was a big-time rock star and a huge commodity for the city. All he had to do was say he was quitting the band to bring about enough pressure on the boffins to accept the children. Maybe?"

Rizzo didn't feel so confident about her assumptions. Confidence was waning in all areas of late for her. Nothing was turning out right and everything seemed skewed somehow. The history, her history wasn't how she remembered it. Too many anomalies and inconsistencies drew her to the conclusion that nothing would be the same from that point on. History was remaking itself. Perhaps the cataclysm wouldn't eventuate?

Dream on. This sort of fantasising is getting us nowhere. You convinced me that it was real. You convinced Henry that it was real. Now you're trying to convince us that it isn't?

"Don't you dare mention that scum bag to me! That filth will get what's coming to him, I swear. Later, though. Time to get somewhere. Time to get schooled up on home birthing too. Maybe one of those pool births? They're said to be pretty good with nice warm water."

And how is this going to come about without funds?

"Did you notice the safe when he replaced those papers?"

Huh?

"The safe in Henry's office? Bet I know the combo."

You mean his birth date?

"Pfft! And you think you're so smart. What does Henry see himself as? Something he takes a measure of comedic pride in?"

Being a volcanologist?

"Half right. He couples that with his other passion, being a Trekkie. So, he likes to claim that he is a...?"

Vulcanologist!

"Correct. And the best-known Vulcan's birth date, Spock, was revealed in a deleted Star Trek scene as being star-date 2230.06!"

You're going to steal?

"Bloody oath! I intend to make that bastard pay two ways from Sunday for what he did."

What he did? You mean when he gave you exactly what you wanted...wrapped up in a more convenient package as twins this time around? How evil of him.

"You're defending him?"

No. Trying to give you a reality check. His kids first time around most likely. His kids second time around. That was your goal, wasn't it?

"It's disgusting and wrong."

And yet exactly what you wanted. You have your children without having to go through the whole wife-bashing thing and consequent car crash. Yay! You won.

"Do you have any more of Daddy's gold nuggets hanging around for us to sell? Any cash squirrelled away under a pillow or mattress somewhere?"

No.

"Rhetorical question. I know you don't have any of that. Other than holding up a bank I have no idea how we go about surviving the next eight months until the babies are born. Any bright ideas?"

Henry?

"That's right, Henry. He has a paternal obligation to uphold."

He's bound to have improved his security since we were there.

"No, he's a creature of pure habit and hates personal change with a passion. As for the hidden cameras, we'll have to disable them."

How?

"Simple. We take out his electricity."

Won't his safe be untouchable in the event of a power failure?

"Jeez, way to find negatives. No, it has a built-in battery backup."

And you know this, how?

"Observation, my dear Rachelle, simple observation. Weren't you watching when he returned those papers?"

When did I get to know about safes? I had no idea what I was looking at.

"It's amazing all the things your mind wanders to when you're cooped up in a hospital bed for a year. I spent so long on the internet I began to feel I was part of it. I researched everything including safes. His was a fairly standard model. If I didn't feel confident that I knew the combination I wouldn't have bothered thinking about it. Pretty tough to get around it any other way. Besides, I don't want to make a scene. In, out and off with my ill-gotten bounty."

Thought you said it would be a righteous bounty?

"Ill-gotten sounds so much more adventurous and daring."

You're enjoying this.

"A chance to stick it to the man? You betcha! First blood."

I think he can make that claim, not you.

"Ouch!"

FIFTEEN

The following months were a hazardous and hectic affair, interspersed with long periods of boredom. It seemed like Rizzo was never able to settle properly in one destination. She would be sitting quietly at a table with her morning coffee, one hand resting on her growing 'bump' when her cup would shatter suddenly from an assailant's bullet missing her by a hair's breadth.

Holed up in a ramshackle abode on the outskirts of Brisbane in Caboolture one time, the Pop Bureau raided the house next door in the early hours of the morning. Someone had tipped off the bureau that a pregnant woman was seen alone. It was only pure luck that the bureau raided the wrong house.

The police were after her for crimes of theft. Henry had called the police after discovering his safe had been burgled. After fingerprints were found, her name was revealed as the perpetrator. Henry was livid and determined in his effort to have her hunted down and locked up.

The unknown assailant managed to find her more than once, though how, became a real conundrum. It didn't seem to matter how well Rizzo covered her tracks, she always ended up being located by one party or another. Eight long months skulking around and finding new accommodations in worsening locations. The bump continued to make movements awkward and painful. Twins, all out front, threatened to topple her if she moved without leaning way back like she was walking down a steep hill.

In a stolen EV, she eventually found her way up into a mountain retreat, a long-term holiday rental on the top of Mt Glorious. A wonderful little rustic shack called *Turkey's Nest*. An idyllic location nestled among tall conifers, semi-rainforest hardwoods and enormous tree ferns. It was nearing the end of her term and her energy was waning considerably. She believed she had covered her tracks, leaving the stolen EV a few kilometres away under an old bridge where it would be washed away with the next tropical downpour.

The shack was rented under a false name and all the transactions took place online through a pre-paid phone without any face-to-face contact. The key was kept in a key safe situated to the right of the main door with the combination issued once the cash was deposited into the owner's post office box.

The added benefit of a heated spa was the clincher for Rizzo when she was searching for likely locations to hole up. Unfortunately, the spa was located outdoors, which meant that her screams during childbirth might attract attention. It would mean that she'd have to bear her burden as silently as possible. Having had the experience of two births already in her earlier life, neither of which she remembered, she wasn't overly confident achieving her goals for a silent birth.

A small supply of painkillers, surgical sutures and a well-stocked first-aid kit allowed her to be as prepared as she might be for the ordeal to come. The body she was in had not previously given birth, so it would not be an easy one, she supposed. All in all, she wasn't in bad shape as long as she remained under the radar. Although the small township on the top of Mt Glorious was a very popular day-trip destination for the people of Brisbane, the cooler weather and persistent rain kept them at bay for a time. Besides, *Turkey's Nest* was well hidden and a considerable distance from the township.

The discomfort Rizzo felt while waddling about on the steep slopes outside her hut, was greatly ignored when she inhaled the fresh mountain air and exotic fragrances, surrounded by a pristine forest dripping with dew in the early mornings after the fog lifted. The heady atmosphere assured Rizzo that she had made the right choice and might approach the owner with a view to purchasing the property with her substantial ill-gotten gains. Who knew Henry had close to half a million dollars tucked away in that safe?

A hefty down payment could be made as a deposit on the hut and Rizzo would then have to find a means of supporting herself and paying off the balance, while rearing twins...no big deal? Right! Coming back down to earth, Rizzo recalled little problem issues connected to that scenario like having to sign contracts and, solicitors getting involved, taxes and stamp duties to be paid with the purchase of property, all while trying to stay under the legal radar? Impossible. Renting the property long-term had to remain her choice for the foreseeable future and stay hidden at all costs.

Going on the run with a pair of babies in tow would be difficult.

Her memories of the never-ending nappy-changes and feedings in the middle of the night were non-existent, but she was intelligent enough to know all that would come crashing down with double the trouble arriving.

It had been exhilarating for Rizzo in her new body, feeling trim, taught and terrific, then the bump came all too soon, reducing her bladder to a flat balloon most nights, causing her to rush to the loo at all hours. Incontinence pads were not something Rizzo though to purchase, however, all too often her mad dash ended before she reached the outdoor loo.

It was a composting toilet set just a little way from the hut so as not to allow the stink too near. Just a metal can with a plastic seat situated over a deep hole in the ground. Add a little sawdust after the deed was done and that was it. Yuck! It was the worst part of being there but her options were limited. No sewerage and no septic tank that far from the town. The steep gradient of the mountainside on which the hut nested precluded large trucks from entering the property to deliver large items like septic tanks and such. Creek water supplied all the drinking water she required.

Solar panels situated on a clearing at the top of the slope provided enough energy for the few necessities, with proficient batteries storing the excess when the sun was hidden behind rain clouds. The spa was heated by propane while the jets were powered by solar electricity. Most afternoons saw Rizzo stripping naked to enter the spa after it was sufficiently heated. The near weightlessness afforded her a welcome relief from the abdominal burden that threatened to topple her with every step she took. The balancing act was not only precarious but exhausting.

On clear nights, through the leafy canopy, Rizzo stared up at the Milky Way in all its glory without the hindrance of city lights, mesmerised as she basked in the warm jets washing over her aching body. It was cool enough for a log fire in her pot-belly stove inside the hut. The owners had ensured there was a ready supply of split timber under a shelter situated next to the outhouse. A smelly trip to and from the wood store, to be sure, but a gratifying outcome when the heat permeated the hut, and the sweet smell of burning wood filled her nostrils. Rizzo recalled her days with her father on those long camping-fossicking trips, allowing her the experience to light a log fire properly.

Another benefit of the isolation and relative comfort was the connections and images she regained partially. Not all of her memories were wiped cleanly and if she concentrated she discovered more.

After fleeing one location after another for months, the reprieve from the relentless pursuit left Rizzo breathless with joy and fulfilment. Just her and soon, her children...

And me!

"Oh, are you still there? I didn't know."

How could you know? You haven't spoken to me in how long?

"Nothing left to say. I know everything you know already."

That's not fair, Rizzo. I'm...scared. I'm...lonely.

"Oh, boo-hoo. If you weren't being so judgmental all the time and sitting high on your bloody high horse, I might make more of an effort. At the moment, you're killing my moment of joy here. Look at this night, would you? Bloody perfect and soooo relaxing," said Rizzo laying back further to rest her head on the outside edge of the spa.

The only sound was the bubbling water in the spa. The forest had gone to sleep with nary a night bird to announce the end of the long day. The stars shone through the canopy and a waxing moon managed to cast a silvery sheen over the tranquil scene. Halfway through a relaxing breath, it struck! The first of the cramps signifying the beginning of labour.

Shit! Is that...? What? What do we do?

"You calm the fuck down is what you do. This isn't my first rodeo remember? I didn't plan for this moment to arrive right now, but we'll take it as it comes. I can't go back inside for the painkillers or anything else I managed to bring with us...damn it! Who knows how long your young body will take to push these watermelons out?"

Do you have to mention watermelons? Is that...is that what it's going to feel like?

"Exactly what it's like. Think of it like shitting a watermelon and you'll get the picture. Same pain, probable tearing, different location."

Gross!

"You have no idea. Giving birth is just the start of everything that gets gross in the world. Shitty nappies are almost insignificant.

When the little pricks suddenly piss, shit or throw up in your mouth, then you know what gross is."

Thought you couldn't remember your children?

"Snippets and random images popping up from time to time."

The cramps became regular just like Rizzo recalled from her extensive research on birthing. The warm water kept her comfortable for the time being. A warmer sensation between her legs heralded the release of her waters. A grimace was all the cramps emitted from the woman at the beginning. After an hour, the strain was telling and the pain was horrific. Managing, barely, to contain her screams, whimpering, Rizzo breathed through the worst of it as she'd been taught by the books.

That fucking hurts! Jeez, Rizzo, do something. I can fucking feel that.

"Knock it off. The last thing I need right now is a cry-baby in my head making me feel worse. What exactly do you expect me to do about it? We're having babies and they decide the timetable. We're just along for the ride and I can't just get up now to go get an aspirin. Suck it up like I'm doing. I have to otherwise I'll scream my head off and someone will hear it out here at night."

Oh, fuck! Oh, Jesus-fucking-Christ. Oh...

"Stop screaming in my head! Yes, it hurts. I told you it would. How are you even feeling it? Thought you lost sensations when I took over? Now stop all that up there and let me concentrate on breathing. It isn't even so bad yet. We haven't begun to shit those watermelons."

The hours wore on, the night air grew cold and the pain intensified. Managing to stifle the yelps of extreme agony that assailed her, Rizzo battled on stoically, resolved to silence the pure terror she felt. Around midnight, the first of the twins slipped through into the warm water and Rizzo's waiting hands. Barely a moment later, the second baby was flushed from her body, followed after a time by the placental expulsion, indicating the third stage of labour was finished.

Exhausted, wounded and breathless, Rizzo laid back with her infants clutched tightly to her chest, their little heads barely above the water. The tiny, red and wrinkled creatures mewled softly as they also battled the fatigue of childbirth. Their rude introduction to a new world was softened greatly by the warm water, so reminiscent of the womb surrounding them.

O.M.G! I can't believe how incredibly ugly they are.

"Welcome to motherhood. I must be connecting misaligned synapses or something because I'm getting more and more memories back. Yep, a pair of faces only a mother could love. They grow on you after a time...like a year, I think. Congratulations Rachelle, you are the proud mother of twins, a boy and a girl. Gabrielle and Lorenzo - meet your mummy. I'm Rachelle and you will not have the surname of Rizzoli. In this body, I'm still Rachelle Shaw so that's the name you guys will have," announced Rizzo with a tired smile.

A small shiver reminded Rizzo that she still had much to do, not the least of which was severing the umbilicals on both children. With nothing on hand, and being unable to transport them all including the afterbirth out of the tub, she was left with little choice but to bite through the tough chords. Clothes pegs she quickly stole from the outdoor clothesline were secured to the severed ends protruding from the babies.

Inside the hut, Rizzo set about building a new fire in the pot-belly after wrapping her bundles in coddling blankets once they were dry. Rizzo had not yet managed to dress and was soon shivering with the cold and the shock of the physical trauma to her body. Without waiting to see if the fire took properly, she ended up collapsing on her bed with her precious babies held close, falling into a deep and uncomfortably painful sleep, with a contented smile etched on her features.

A whirlwind of activity consumed her waking and sleeping hours over the following weeks. It was double the strain of a single birth with each twin waking the other and feeding off each other's stress. The cries of hungry children seemed to blur into an endless session of feeding, burping and nappy changing, with only a moment or two for a quick nap and a bite to eat in between. Her eyes bulged from their sockets as the pair woke at all hours, driving Rizzo to distraction and delirium.

The first night's full sleep did not come soon enough for Rizzo's liking. The bliss of those first uninterrupted hours worked wonders on her aching soul. So quiet was the pair, that Rizzo woke alarmed that something was dreadfully wrong. It was pure relief to see them huddled together and gurgling happily in their bassinettes, playing with their toes. The smell assailing her nostrils told Rizzo that all was not the happy scene it seemed.

Oh, that is just disgusting!

"Hah! Wait till they're on solids. This is nothing yet."

When does the good stuff start? I thought motherhood was about happy smiling babies and laughing and playing?

"That all comes much later. After the teething, it starts to become more congenial. Until then, this is about as good as it gets. Enjoy these moments when there's peace in the house. Feeding time is usually the only time we get to have some quiet. Sitting in our rocking chair with a baby at each breast sucking away. Ah, so wonderful."

Ugh, can't believe you want all that.

"Don't you feel the connection, that inalienable bond that only a mother can experience? It's more than even a spiritual connection, it's physical, tangible. Yes, I want all that. Everything I've done to get to this point has been worth it. I have my babies back. My children that were taken from me by that mongrel...whose name I still can't remember."

What are you talking about?

"The one who sent me back. The one who forced my children in that timeline to take their lives. I might not know exactly what they looked like, what their personalities were like, or anything other than a welling deep down inside of me, but I know them. And the bastard will pay who took them away from me."

Won't be a world left if we don't do something about stopping the cataclysm.

"Who knows if it will happen this time around? Things are already different."

Complacency? Not like you. Besides, we have killers, the Bureau and the cops after us!

"All the more reason to stay here under the radar."

Then their world erupted!

SIXTEEN

A phalanx of armour-clad troops had broken down the front door after surrounding the mountain hideout. Rizzo and her babies were separated and taken into custody, transported down the mountain to an unknown destination in separate vehicles. Even restrained, Rizzo managed to cause no end of problems for her captors, cursing, struggling, and spitting her venom at the cowards who took her babies away.

The windows on the van had been blacked out, leaving her with no idea where they might be taking her, other than downwards, which she knew once her ears popped. It was assumed by Rizzo that they were headed towards the city, and the dreaded Pop Bureau, not known for their compassion or sympathy.

So much for flying under the radar!

The smarmy comment from her head-rider caused Rizzo to fume inwardly. Rachelle Shaw wasn't helping the situation. Not for the first time did Rizzo wonder why she retained the presence of her younger interloper. According to the theory, Rizzo should have taken over completely without a trace of the former personality. It should have happened months ago. Nothing was turning out the way it should have.

The van took a few sudden turns before descending into a hollow-sounding area, an underground parking lot, she assumed. The sliding door on the van was opened from the outside by two burly troopers dressed in full assault armour and weaponry, wearing dark aviator glasses to hide their eyes. Motioning for their prisoner to alight in the direction of a well-lit pair of sliding glass doors, Rizzo refused to budge.

"Fuck you, and the horse you rode in on. Where are my children?"

The lead trooper then levelled his assault rifle directly at Rizzo's face after 'loading one in the slot', as his comrade put it.

"Are you kidding? You're willing to shoot me over a breach of the birthing policy? What are we back in Nazi Germany?"

"Dr Rachelle Rizzoli, you have exactly five seconds to comply with my orders or you will never see your children alive again. You are to march through those doors ahead of us, without any further comments or delay. I am authorised to injure you in any way I see fit. My first bullet will enter your kneecap. A particularly painful injury, one which I will repeat on your other knee if the need arises. I will continue with elbows, wrists, ankles and such, until you have no limbs left, if necessary, but remain alive."

The unfeeling automaton called her by her future name! That was a game-changer. It was clear that Rizzo was dealing with more than just the Pop Bureau. Something far more sinister was at play and she had to watch her tongue from that moment forward. The lives of her children were at stake. There was nothing she wouldn't do for them, including playing nice for the time being.

"Seeing as you put it so nicely, lead on, McDuff," she said, unaware of the odd quip's origins.

Everything about you is odd, lady!

Escorting her down a long hallway leading to an elevator, the troopers shoved her inside roughly then pushed a button for the one hundred and forty-fifth floor. When the doors finally opened after what seemed an eternity of electronic music, the silent guards pushed her forward. Along yet another hallway that led to an enormous office overlooking the city of Brisbane.

It was relatively early in the morning. The sun managed to peek through the smog already settling on the skyline. The huge corner office was a great example of minimalist decor. White and stainless steel with the odd splash of colour on the wall in the way of an abstract painting that any two-year-old might have managed. A very pretty, immaculately-dressed, polished man rose from his glass desk in front of the floor to ceiling windows overlooking the city. He greeted the small party.

"Ah, so glad you could join us, Dr Rizzoli. Do you know who I am?"

"A dead man if I get the chance," she replied in a cold tone.

"Good, you don't know me then. I feared you might, in which case you would probably be hostile towards me," the man tittered at his joke.

The insouciant and frivolous manner of the effeminate man stirred an emotion in Rizzo without any direct knowledge of its foundation.

"You have made a right royal mess of things, Doctor Rizzoli.

You had a mission to prevent the cataclysm. Your mission was to make contact with Dr Thoms and stop him from going ahead with his plans. Of course, you never should have made it that far. I sent back at least two others to end your rotten existence and they failed," said the man as he sashayed his way back to the desk while his troopers nudged Rizzo to follow.

"Mind telling me who you are and what this is all about?"

"You genuinely don't know me? Don't recognise me?" asked the man as he sat behind the desk, gesturing for Rizzo to sit in front.

"Should I?"

"No, not at all. Those memories were wiped but we had no idea how successful we would be."

"You, you called me Doctor Rizzoli. You're from..."

"The future, yes. My name is Karl Shadforth, PA to the Minister for Energy, a flunky, in this timeline. I had to make the journey back in time myself to make sure the mission was proceeding as planned. You were supposed to be dead, not playing mummy to a couple of bloody ankle-biters. How have you managed to avoid being dead, I wonder?"

"I...don't understand..."

"Nor should you. Nor do I give a fig that you do or don't. The whole idea was to appease the other directors of Under-City Australis by sending you back under the pretence of correcting the calamity. The incompetent assassins I sent back failed. You then fucked up royally. You convinced Thoms about the fact that you were from the future. You planted the bloody seed that someone messed with his fucking drill which caused the cataclysm."

"You...you wanted me dead? You don't...didn't want me to prevent the cataclysm? Or..."

"Of course I didn't want you to prevent the bloody cataclysm. How else do you think I came to power? My successful businesses notwithstanding, I was nothing but a glorified secretary to the Minister for Energy until the world went to shit. Now I've had to come back to be his bootlicker again for a while until all that shit repeats itself. All because you couldn't simply do as you were told. I warned those idiots that you were too unstable for the mission, that your rotten children would see you make mistakes. Why would you even think you could recreate them? Are you a complete moron? Your memories of those shits were wiped, how did you know about them?"

"You left the emotions there. The instinct to be a mother was far stronger than your memory wipe. I even managed a snippet or two of those memories. Just fragments. You caused the death of my children in the future, now you're doing it here."

"I had nothing to do with that. They took their own lives to take away the obstacle to you accepting the mission."

"So, all this...was an elaborate ruse? Just so you could get off on a little power trip?"

"Head Director for Under-City Australis is no small power trip, as you so inadequately put it. I became the leader of a new generation, a new system of government, a new existence below ground. Only one thing was preventing my complete victory. Your little password you blackmailed us all with. Without that encrypted input each year the power goes off and everyone dies. So, the plan was simple. You go back. You fail in your mission to prevent the cataclysm. You die from an assassin's bullet and I replicate the drill design to produce the power for Under-City Australis instead of you and no longer require that bloody password to keep everything going."

"You're totally off your nut. A complete whacko! Aren't you forgetting the air purifiers? You were all going to die anyway! What's the point of all this if it all goes ahead the same way?"

"Oh, you're just as dense now as you were then. I simply have them install better filters which we can reach and replace at will. The problem with the way it was is that the tunnels were collapsed and we had no way of reaching the surface to replace the filters if we had the spares. I'll make sure that is resolved. Only, you've made it so no one can get at Dr Thom's device now. He's fallen off the face of the planet with his designs, prototypes, the lot."

"What has that got to do...?"

"It was me. I headed up the private conglomerate that hired him back then. I was the one to put him on the drilling platform on the bottom of the trench. When I heard of his drill and what it could do, I wasted no time in snavelling him up for the private consortium I financed. I wasn't about to spend my life toadying up to that buffoon of an energy minister. Using me in that way while his wife thought he was so straight and faithful! Oh puh-lease! Now, seeing as bloody Thoms can't be found and convinced to alter his precious little drill to do what I want it to do, then it's up to you. *You* are going to manufacture the drill."

"Don't be ridic..."

"Don't try my patience. I have your children and won't hesitate to end their lives or cause them extreme pain if you refuse."

"What makes you think I can duplicate the design?"

"You already have, remember, in a few years from now?"

"You want me to recreate the drill from pure memory alone, with the flaw, just so you can cause the cataclysm...again?"

"Exactly."

"Fat chance. If we're all going to die anyway, why would I?"

"You don't have to perish and neither do your children. I could arrange for that."

"I have no guarantee of that. You're not a man...thing...to be trusted. You're a sadistic lunatic..."

The sound of distressed crying permeated the office.

"Hear that? That's the sound of hungry infants crying out for their mother's milk. I'm happy to let you hear them like that until they can no longer make those ghastly sounds until they starve slowly to death?"

Rizzo blanched at hearing her babies' cries coming from the overhead speakers, her resolve breaking instantly. Reluctantly, she nodded her agreement to the young man in the bespoke suit and evil grin.

"I warn you; any more resistance and you will lose one of them. Take her away so she can feed the horrors, then separate them again. I will speak to you the moment you're finished."

Accompanying the troopers, Rizzo shut her mouth to the insult balanced on the tip of her tongue. The time would come, she promised, when Karl Shadforth would pay for his sins in the present and the future. For the time being, she had to play along to keep her children and herself alive. At the end of the long bland hallway, Rizzo was shoved into a bare white room where her children cried from their bassinettes resting on the floor.

They were quick to quieten the moment she gave them succour, Rizzo resting on the only piece of furniture in the windowless room. The hard, plastic chair with high armrests was very uncomfortable and entirely unconducive to breastfeeding. Struggling to make it work as best she could, Rizzo found her centre, that place of peace and harmony while feeding her babies.

What the fuck was all that about?

"I'm sure you can figure it out."

That was the prick that sent you back in time?

"I don't remember, but it feels about right."

They wiped your memories of him?

"Something like that."

Charming. What are we going to do?

"We are going to do everything in our power to ensure the lives of my children."

At the cost of billions of other lives worldwide?

"Yep. I don't give a fuck about them. No one gave a damn about me, even when I provided them with clean energy after the shit hit the fan. I was ostracised and vilified, tried and found guilty for my efforts. The world can go fuck itself."

What about me?

"What about you? You're existing on borrowed time already. You shouldn't be up there."

Well, I am here and I don't want to die or disappear. I haven't lived my life yet and I worked damn hard to get where I am. You can't do what he's asking. Henry had enough sense to disappear, knowing that he was outnumbered.

"How exactly do you think I can accomplish that task, hmm? I'm trapped in that lunatic's ivory tower and I have two babies who are wholly dependent on me."

Pfft! Nothing a wet nurse can't provide.

"I've already lost my children. I don't intend to let that happen again. Look, I don't even think I can build their stupid drill from scratch. It's not a simple design by any stretch of the imagination. My memory is pretty fragged after all that they've done to me. I don't think I could do it even if I wanted to. Then there's the whole 'doing it wrong thing'? They want me to replicate the flawed design, not the one I managed to repair."

Great! That's good news. No drill. No cataclysm. Yay!

"If I don't begin building something that maniac will start torturing me and my children. I still can't believe the idiot wants me to bring about the apocalypse. All for a power trip, so he can head the Committee of Directors governing UCA. What sort of an upbringing did he have to turn him into that sort of demented, evil shit?"

You're going into nurture versus nature with that question and quite frankly, I think he was born that way. You can't turn somebody into that.

"Regardless, I have to convince him that I'm doing what he wants. I don't mind admitting that my head's spinning at the moment. This is...complicated."

No shit? Think how I feel.

"So, this Karl Shadforth was the PA for the energy minister when the shit went down. He had access to the first communications between Dr Thoms and the Department of Energy. He sees the potential for huge money in green energy and starts his consortium of investors to create a company that employs Dr Thoms, leading him away from the government. Henry says his design has no flaws, and I tend to agree with him. How does it get fucked up? Something doesn't add up here."

You do realise they're probably listening right now?

"Fuck! I didn't think..."

Shit!

"One-sided conversation, though. Who cares? Hope they left me some nappies."

Rizzo spent the next half hour changing the babies and settling them into sleep when the door was unlocked from the outside.

"Mr Shadforth would like to see you again, ma'am," explained the trooper from before, with the same detached expression and sunglasses."

"You do realise you're indoors, right?" quipped Rizzo as she walked past the humourless man.

"Ah, Dr Rizzoli, I assume you've had a moment to reconsider your situation in a more congenial light?" Asked Karl with a shit-eating grin.

"Don't see that I have a lot of choices," Rizzo admitted.

"Excellent. In that case, I'll have you flown to a secret laboratory my investors and I have set up just outside the city. You will find everything you require to begin building the laser drill...including the flaw. You were correct in assuming we were listening, though who you could have been talking to is a mystery. Care to enlighten us?"

"Care to go and get fucked?"

"Charming to the last, aren't we? Well, I don't care what you think of me as long as you do as you're told. Deviate from that path one iota, and you will lose one of your children. No warnings, no second chances. Do I make myself crystal clear?"

"Who determines that?"

"What do you mean?"

"I'm dealing with a shaky memory at best to come up with a replica of someone else's design for an immensely complicated and sophisticated apparatus. Who is going to judge whether I am adhering to the design or not? Who is going to have the expertise to make a judgment call on my progress or lack thereof? I mean, we are talking about a little experimentation along the way, a little bit of trial and error? I'd hate for some idiot to make a false assumption on my work and end up losing one of the children over their erroneous report to you."

"I will follow your progress personally. You will report directly and only to me."

"You?"

"Yes."

"You wouldn't know your arse from your elbow."

"I have an appropriate understanding of the principle involved."

"An appropriate... It takes a helluva lot more than a bit of an understanding of the principles involved to make informed decisions about the reports I'd send."

"Not your concern. I'll know if..."

"No, you won't. You haven't had the experience or the education to make heads or tails of the complex code and schematics required for the laser drill. *I* had difficulty following much of Dr Thoms' information."

"Well then, you'd better make damn sure that I *can* understand your reports. You will understand if I require you to be blindfolded for the trip to the secret location?"

"That won't be necessary..."

"It will be of absolute necessity, I'm afraid. I won't have any more slip-ups and I won't be taking any chances of the location becoming public knowledge. You won't have access to communication devices but as I said, I won't be taking any chances."

"Wait! I have to have access to the internet, at least. It will be imperative to the work."

"You will have to relay the information you require via one of my attendants who will be assisting you. I understand you've met her, Cordelia? She was only a botanist in her future life but I'm sure she'll be handy for you."

"I knew she couldn't be trusted."

"Oh, I wouldn't be too unkind about her. She was being held to ransom much like yourself. Another pathetic woman who would do anything to protect the life of her sprog. Stupid of her to let you go and now she'll have to make up for that slip. All she had to do was kill you and she could have spent the rest of her days happily smothering that rotten child of hers in sloppy affection. As a reward for her failure, she will now have to assist you. I'm also supplying you with a nanny to care for your brats while you're working. I can't have you wasting your valuable time with nappy changes and all that cooing nonsense. You may continue to breastfeed them unless I see you falter in your duties. Treasure those times as that is all you'll be allowed to have with them."

"You can't be serious?"

"Serious as a heart attack. Care to test my resolve?" menaced Karl with a look of steely determination.

SEVENTEEN

"**Are you positive** this is the only way?"

"We aren't dealing with absolutes here, no guarantees. We're talking about psychological probabilities."

"It's taking far too long and is getting too bloody complex!"

"It's new ground and we have no points of reference. If we try to rush it, we may do irreversible damage."

"It should have been...wait...is that...shit!"

"Oh, it wasn't...I mean...sleep...mode..."

EIGHTEEN

Snippets of the strange dream conversation stayed with Rizzo as she awoke. The blackness surrounding her seemed strange, almost material-like until she remembered the hood placed over her head for transportation to the secret laboratory. Removal of the hood allowed Rizzo to take in her new surroundings, a fully-equipped laboratory with a simple cot from which she rose. There were no windows and a strange quality to the air she couldn't identify. There was also a muted hum coming from somewhere. Outside the laboratory, she heard hollow, metallic sounds.

Figuring she had fallen asleep during the journey, Rizzo stood to explore her new quarters. She found all manner of electronic componentry along with the fundamentals for building a computer and a working monitor on which she presumed she would soon be forced to build the complex code required for running the laser. A small bar fridge housed bottled water and basic pre-packaged food, mainly sandwiches.

Feeling hungry, Rizzo ripped open a pack of ham and salad sandwiches and munched quietly. Her breasts felt heavy and leaked slightly, indicating feeding time for her babies was overdue. The metallic hatch opened as she was thinking those thoughts. A strange woman she had never seen before approached her silently with two wrapped bundles in her arms. The mawkish woman with a pinched face handed over the babies silently before exiting through the hatch.

Hatch! It was an oval hatch. Were they on a ship? Before Rizzo could ponder the new information, her babies were squirming in her arms, about to let loose with manic squalls unless they were given sustenance. Settling herself on the cot once more, Rizzo lost herself to the pleasant routine.

Who's the old crone and where the fuck are we?

"My guess is we're on a ship, though we must be docked because I can't feel any motion. There's a hum in the background, so it could be the diesel motors. Must be a pretty big ship, I reckon."

You're awfully calm, considering.

"Worrying or panicking isn't going to help us. I guess the old woman was the nanny he spoke of? Charming old dragon."

Reminds me of the witch from Hansel and Gretel. Got the nose for it.

"I had the oddest dream before I woke up. Sounded so real. I heard voices talking about something. Didn't get the gist of what they were talking about, though. Did you hear something?"

Did I hear your dream? I know I'm in your head but I can't hear or see your dreams, Rizzo. I can hear your thoughts loud enough.

"I'm...kind of glad you're here with me."

First time you've shown a shred of interest in me. Scared, are you?

"Concerned. I don't know if I can do what's being asked of me...or if I should. What would you do?"

Play for time. Make out like a busy little beaver doing stuff that has the right appearance, all while keeping an eye out for an opportunity to get away, I suppose.

"If we're on a ship, what chance do we have of finding a way off or away...with two babies?"

Lifeboat?

"Great. Adrift in the middle of the ocean somewhere until we die of dehydration or drown in some squall."

You said that we were probably moored? We might be nowhere near an ocean. Tied up in a marina or a calm inlet.

"What a fucking mess!"

Half an hour later the hatch opened again to allow the old woman to enter.

"Do you have a name?" Rizzo asked, attempting to keep hold of her babies.

The woman, who refused to answer, held out her hands for the babies with a scowl on her face.

"Where are you taking them? Where are we?" asked Rizzo in a mild panic.

Two armed guards entered with weapons drawn, aimed straight at Rizzo. Reluctantly, Rizzo handed over the babies. They soon exited without a word spoken. Ensuring the hatch was locked, Rizzo fumed over the lack of information and her prisoner status.

"I suggest you get to work, Dr Rizzoli or the next feeding time will be delayed by an hour," announced the voice over the speaker in the ceiling.

It wasn't clear who the voice belonged to. It may have been Shadforth, but Rizzo couldn't be sure. The speaker had a tinny quality to it that disguised the owner. Somewhere outside the laboratory, a loud clang could be heard. To Rizzo, it sounded like a tool being dropped on a metal gangplank, echoing throughout the ship. A ship? A sudden thought had Rizzo sweating. Though she felt sure the ship was securely at anchor or moored to a jetty, it was still a ship. That meant it could be moved. Moved to...

"Shit. You don't suppose they'd be stupid enough to take us to the Bougainville Trench?"

Seems likely, considering they want to recreate the cataclysm. You said that's where it happened?

"According to the best knowledge and the recovered flotation safe. When Henry Thoms used the drill aboard the *Bougainville Bess*, it started the chain reaction that set the ring of fire alight with hundreds of volcanoes erupting at once. Below and above the water. That underwater drilling platform was the first casualty of the cataclysm."

I don't get it. Henry isn't an idiot and you said his designs were good. What could have happened? Why would he intentionally...

"Sabotage his own work? He wouldn't. It was his baby. It was going to change the world, give easy access to unlimited energy. No way would that conceited prick deliberately fuck up. His ego wouldn't allow it."

So?

"Someone else got to it. It's the only explanation."

"Dr Rizzoli! While I do not have listening devices situated in the laboratory, I do have visual capabilities. What I am seeing is a whole lot of nothing happening after I just gave you an order to begin. Do not test my patience. You and your mongrel brats will regret any deviation from my instructions."

Rizzo glared up at the speaker located on the ceiling. A small lens with a blinking red light revealed the camera keeping tabs on her movements. It was very clear, that time, who the voice belonged to...Shadforth! Whether he was aboard the ship or viewing her remotely, she couldn't guess. Either way, she would have to begin the task she had been assigned. With no clue as to her ability to deliver, Rizzo began to inspect all the equipment around her.

Without a clear understanding of how or why, Rizzo began to assemble and craft together many of the electrical components. The basic design for the laser drill was centred on a Gatling gun principle, whereby a series of lasers were shot out of a central hub at incredible speeds in rotation. The angle of the lasers, aimed inward, would essentially vaporise the substrate through which it was aimed. A thermodynamic sleeve was lowered as the drill hole progressed.

It was a very simple overview of a highly complex instrument with a plethora of components, lenses and moving parts. Just the timing on the lasers alone was a daunting proposition requiring many days of experimentation and trials. Though she loathed the reason for her endeavours, she basked in the work, spending hour after hour with her head buried in the readouts and notes, losing track of all time until her babies were brought to her for feeding.

The silent crone, dressed in the same clothes every day, would deliver and pick the children up without showing any signs of emotion. Food was replaced in her fridge every day by the troopers who covered each other with weapons at the ready every step of the way. The days and weeks wore on without Rizzo hearing from her jailor. Grateful to be left alone, she immersed herself in her work, surprised at her daily advances.

How much longer will it take?

"I finished a few days ago."

What?

"Somehow, I managed. Don't ask me how."

I am asking you how?

"I did correct his designs. I recreated the drill to provide UCA with all the energy requirements it needed."

So, what have you been doing for the last couple of days?

"Delaying, playing for time. Only, I don't see a way out. The guards are always covering each other and the old woman. No way to try anything without getting shot. I won't risk the lives of my children."

Did you build it like he asked, with the flaw?

"What choice did I have? I've had to supply him with copies of all my notes and pictures of my prototypes. It wouldn't take a Rhodes Scholar to make sense of them. I'm sure he has a phalanx of lackeys at his disposal to check over the designs and the coding."

If it works, why not use it?

"Are you insane?"

Not in the way he intends to use it. Use it as a weapon. Take out the camera first of all, then aim it at the goons when they come rushing in to find out what happened to the live feed.

"There aren't any safeguards, no limiters in place."

Doesn't matter. The first shot is up through the top of the ship and into the sky after that. The only worry is that a passing plane would be unlucky enough to be overhead. When you aim it at the goons, it will be aimed at the side of the vessel. Unless we're below the waterline, it shouldn't be a concern.

"It stands to reason that we would be below the waterline, surely?"

I don't see why. I don't hear the engines very clearly, which would indicate that we aren't well below decks?

"The engines aren't operating at the moment because we're moored and you're forgetting the babies. I would have to find them and get off the ship. We could be in the middle of the ocean. Even locating and securing a lifeboat would still mean that we are lost at sea."

As far as I can tell, you're out of time. Shadforth will know how far along you are by the reports, yes?

"I suppose," Rizzo admitted reluctantly.

You have to do something very soon, or the opportunity will be taken from you. How long do you think he'll keep those children alive if he has what he asked for?

"But..."

Just do it! Before it's too late.

Rizzo moved to a bench where an instrument looking like a large telescope on a pivoting base sat atop the surface. The device was hooked up to a long line of batteries drawing their power from an unknown source outside the lab. Rizzo swivelled the instrument around and pivoted it up toward the camera on the ceiling. Face contorted into a grimace of glee, Rizzo fired the device nanoseconds before the alarms began.

An unexpected reaction to the silent blast of laser power caught Rizzo off-guard. Water came gushing through the 200mm aperture created by the laser drill. Cold water. Freezing water! No one came through the hatch as expected. Trapped in the locked room with water pouring in through the hole and alarms going off all about her, Rizzo hopped onto the nearest bench to get her bare feet out of the icy water.

"You are either the densest woman who was ever born or the cleverest. You finally worked out where you were, did you? Only now you've sealed the fate of you and your ankle-biters. You didn't accomplish much other than that. I have the designs and I also have a sister vessel to the *Bougainville Belle* in the dry docks ready to be deployed."

"What are you talking about you lunatic? What...? Wait, how can you still be talking and seeing me?"

"Did you think I would rely on just one set of eyes and ears? Yes, you heard right, ears. I've been listening to you blathering on to yourself this whole time. And you think I'm a looney? You lost, Rachelle. I have the designs and you'll be dead within moments either by drowning or by the pressure if the drilling platform doesn't stand up to the damage you've inflicted on it."

"Drilling platform?"

"So you didn't figure it out? I put you somewhere you would never escape from a location that would make you the first casualty of the cataclysm; on The *Bougainville Belle* at the bottom of the trench. If the hull doesn't bear up, you will escape drowning only to be crushed by the enormous pressure of being under an ocean of water. I'll deploy the second drilling platform to your location the moment she's fully functional, which should be any day now and finish what I started."

"You're insane!"

"Am I? I'm not the one who'll be dying shortly. I'll be repeating everything I did to establish myself as the Head Director of UCA once the cataclysm wreaks havoc on the world. It needed a cleansing, Rachelle, you know that. The world would never have sustained the massive over-population or the depletion of all its natural resources. The planet needed to be purged, to allow a fresh beginning. Under-City Australis will emerge into the new reality as a super-power with far fewer lives to pollute and consume."

"Your pathetic attempts at some form of altruism don't fool me. I may not have any memories of you from the future but I can tell what sort of snivelling parasite you are. A megalomaniacal piece of shit. You don't give a rat's arse about the rest of humanity, only that you get to rule."

"Oh, you wound me," he said in a supercilious manner. "I'm going to enjoy watching you die. It will be deeply satisfying to finally see the end of you. I taste victory."

The water had risen dramatically in the short time she had been talking to the maniac. The temperature in the lab had dropped significantly. Thankfully, the alarms had all been switched off, leaving only the sound of the waterfall coming through the hole in the ceiling. With chattering teeth, Rizzo plucked a chair from the water to place it on the bench. She perched herself on top of the chair to get her feet out of the rising waters.

With a sinking feeling in her gut, Rizzo realised that there would be no escape if what Shadforth said was true. The lab was locked from the outside and filling fast with water. Hypothermia would most likely get her first. The temperature of the water at the bottom of the Bougainville trench which had never seen daylight was a mere four degrees Celsius. The pressure would be in the order of a thousand times greater than at sea level.

The harsh glare of the neon lights was replaced by the emergency red lighting, bathing the lab and the rising water in an eerie glow. The temperature was dropping steadily. Rizzo shivered. The water lapped the underside of the office chair on which she perched. It would soon cover the seat.

That water is freaking cold!

"No shit? Tell me something I don't know."

"You really are a freak, Rachelle. Talking to yourself?"

"I'm talking to my younger self, arsehole! She's trapped in my head."

"How extraordinary! My, my, my, aren't we the creative one?"

"I don't know what you're talking about, Shadforth. Why don't you just piss off and let me die in peace."

"And miss the spectacle? The demise of the great Rachelle Rizzoli? Hero of Under-City Australis? Not on your nelly. I wouldn't miss this moment for all the lithium in Australia."

"Hero? Hardly. Thanks to you and your cohorts I was an outcast. An object of pure derision. Ahh!"

"Cold, isn't it? Hypothermia soon. Then you'll probably just give in to it by relaxing and accepting your fate, to go gently into that good night."

The water had reached over the chair's seat. Rizzo knelt on it, her face reaching the cold, metal bulkhead. There was nothing she could do to keep warm or to prevent herself from succumbing to hypothermia. The red ambience flickered briefly. Complete darkness brought on a mini panic attack, but the red light came back on soon after.

"Out of curiosity, seeing as it makes no difference anymore, what did you use to encrypt the computer controlling the thermodynamic flow in UCA?"

"Wh-wh-why, w-w-would I tell you th-th-at?"

"Like I said, just curiosity. I can't get back to that future anymore and I have the plans for the device now so the encryption becomes superfluous."

Rizzo felt the first signs of hypothermia permeating her body, slowing down with the extreme cold. The air was thinning considerably in the space that remained between the ceiling and the surface of the water, lapping her chin. Her mind threatened to shut down her pain receptors and her consciousness along with it.

May as well tell the idiot. Show him how smart you are.

"Fib-F-Fibonacci Sequence," whispered Rizzo as the water dribbled into her mouth, heralding her demise.

"Our number boffins were at it for ages..."

"Al-al-alphabet...start at zero."

"You mean it begins with... Um, that would be...A - B - B - C - D - F - I? Like that? How long?"

"Ahh...C-c-cold!"

"How long, Rachelle? How many iterations?"

"My-my-my..." Rizzo couldn't complete the answer as the water rose above her mouth."

NINETEEN

"Her age! She had to have meant her age. She was thirty, wasn't she? Try that many iterations using the letter A as first a zero, then a twenty-six value and so on. Hold the simulation until we know for sure."

Rizzo listened to the disembodied voice echoing around her with fascination. Blackness surrounded her, though the debilitating cold was no longer an issue. She felt very strange and, disconnected, incomplete somehow, like coming out of a nightmare.

"Well? Do we have it?" asked Shadforth impatiently.

"We have it," answered the other voice triumphantly. The file is accessible.

"It's about bloody time. Cutting it awfully fine, weren't we? What if she'd drowned before we got the information?"

"It had to go that way, Karl. It was the only way she would reveal the encryption if she knew all was lost and she had seconds to live. All the psyche evaluations we did on her pointed to that singular conclusion," answered another voice that Rizzo recognised vaguely as coming from Cordelia.

"Would we have lost her completely if she drowned?"

"Probably not. Just a matter of starting again."

"We have the file open? We have the location?"

"We believe so."

"Do we have it or not?"

"We have the location from the file. No way of knowing for certain if it's the one we're after."

"The correct designs for the drill are on there?"

"Complete with schematics and coding by the look of it."

"Very well, then. Give Henry access to the file and tell him to start construction of the drill immediately."

"Henry's plane hasn't landed yet. He'll be arriving in a few hours."

"Let me know the moment he arrives."

"Karl?"

"What is it?"

"What are going to do with...?"

"Shut it down, wipe it. All of it, no trace remaining."

"What if?"

"What if what? Are you trying to tell me that the information doesn't reveal the site?"

"Wouldn't it be prudent to wait until we have definitive proof?"

"If the file doesn't contain the site information, why would it have been encrypted?"

"I'm just saying it would be advisable to..."

"NO! End it now! I want nothing more to do with that horrible thing."

TWENTY

When Rizzo became aware of her surroundings once more, it came as quite a shock. In front of her sat Cordelia looking straight at her.

"Hello, Rachelle."

"Cordelia?"

"Yes."

"What, what happened? Where am I? Why can't I feel my legs...or my arms?"

"That is a long story, I'm afraid. Be thankful you exist at all. Karl wanted me to shut you down completely and format the drive. I managed to smuggle you out despite all the security measures in place."

"I don't...understand."

"No. I'm sure you don't. Look, I don't expect you to forgive me but I'd like to apologise for everything that's been done to you."

"Can you cut the shit and tell me what's going on. Where am I? What just happened? Am I dead?"

"You were...at least, part of you was...is."

"Fuck! Make sense, would you?"

"Okay, okay. Do you recall the car crash?"

"The one that crippled me? What sort of a stupid question is that? Of course, I remember the bloody car crash!"

"It didn't cripple you, Rachelle. It killed you. At least, your body. We were able to salvage your consciousness, though, with ground-breaking new technology. We uploaded that consciousness into a supercomputer. I'm afraid the transfer to this simple computer of mine won't be anything like you're used to in the other one. That's why you don't feel limbs and such. My computer can't augment your feelings to include a body."

"What are you saying? I don't..."

Rizzo was losing control of her senses. The world spun around. It was impossible to fully grasp the meaning of the words she heard. Dead? In the crash? It had to be a bunch of lies. There didn't seem to be a single logical reason for any of it. Lies? How much of it?

What?

"Rachelle? Hello, Rachelle? Don't go fading on me. I need you to be with me right now. I know it's a lot to take in, but you're a strong woman. You have to come to terms with it or you're doomed. I don't have the expertise to bring you back. My coding skills are barely passable. I was in charge of the psychology of the project. Others were responsible for the insane coding of the construct."

"The...construct?" asked Rizzo settling down some.

"The story we put you through. It was all made up by us to gain the information in that encrypted file of yours."

"So, I'm still in Under-City Australis and it was all a ruse to get me to reveal the encryption for the annual passcode?"

"No, Rachelle. There is no Under-City Australis. It's the year 2149, two years after Lorenzo was born and a year after your horrific accident. Yes, we fudged the dates in your story as well. The airbags cushioned your brain enough for us to rescue your consciousness but not sufficiently to save your body."

"Bullshit!"

Cordelia held up a mirror. Rizzo saw the image of a computer monitor with her face on the screen, nothing else. Rizzo's world came crashing down around her. It was too much. It was an impossible overload, an unbearable avalanche of information barrelling towards her at great velocity.

"Rachelle, you have to calm yourself. Your vital signs are off the charts, spiking at critical levels."

"What fucking vital signs? I have no vital signs. I don't have a body, no..."

"But you have a mind. A brilliant mind which I rescued. If you don't calm down you'll overload the circuits that are keeping your brain alive. Do you understand? You'll fry the electronics keeping your consciousness going. I see the temperature rising as we speak. The internal fans and the exterior air-conditioning won't cope much longer. It's imperative that you cool down...literally."

"I...why?"

"Why do all this? Why keep your brain alive?"

"Yes, why? I don't understand...any of this."

"Doctor Rizzoli, you have no idea what you uncovered."

"What? What are you on about?"

"I know we wiped a lot of your memories but there must be

something still there? The invention you were working on? The laser drill?"

"My...no...Thoms..."

"Dr Thoms is working for Karl's company. He didn't come up with the design for the drill, Rachelle. You did. You were working for the Department of Energy when you began working on a design for the laser drill. That much we know. We also know you did some amateur fossicking at a site you were hoping to make your test site. Then you had the accident and your research was lost. You encrypted your files before the accident. Karl desperately needed the location of that site."

"Why?"

"Karl had fingers in a lot of pies. One of them was in assay testing. Very handy when someone makes a claim. Before they get the results of the test, Karl steps in to purchase the claim if he thinks it's worth his time and money. In your case, well, it was worth every cent of the millions he poured into saving you and building the construct to gain the information he needed. You sent in an unusual rock sample from your fossicking. Why? Why would you need to know what was in the sample? You were hoping to reach a thermal pocket with your drill, not prospecting."

"Had to confirm the geology...I think...I suppose."

"Well, Karl got a hold of the results. If true, the test site could be worth more than Australia's gross earnings for the last hundred years."

"How?"

"You stumbled across a find of monumental implications to someone like Karl Shadforth. Embedded in that rock sample were microscopic crystalline structures which turned out to be blue diamonds, Rachelle, of unparalleled quality, flawless. Worth millions and millions of dollars per carat. The colour and clarity rival the best-known example of a blue diamond, *The Hope Diamond*, found in India. Your samples showed promise of further discoveries and larger gems estimated to be worth trillions. Enough to lure Karl Shadforth into investing a substantial sum of money to save your brain after the accident."

"I'm responsible for the cataclysm?"

"No, Rachelle. Don't you see? It never happened. That was all part of the story we invented after careful psychological evaluation of your history, your personality, and your entrance exams into the department, especially your aptitude tests. Karl had me and a team of psychoanalysts working on it for months to get it right. It had to be elaborate to get you to reveal the encryption code for the file."

"You invented that whole story after the crash? The hospital, the pain and suffering, the abuse I received in the underground city...everything? What sort of a sadistic bunch of evil shits are you? That's..."

"Was the only reason you're ali..."

"Don't you dare say alive, don't you dare! That's despicable."

"I did apologise," said Cordelia weakly, sagging in her chair.

The days, weeks and months spent on the psychology and the construct were finally taking their toll on her. The guilt and the remorse had been eating away at her soul. She knew it was a despicable act, knew she didn't deserve forgiveness but hoped for it just the same. Not only had Doctor Rachelle Rizzoli suffered under the tyranny of a demented individual calling himself her husband, but she had also suffered the physical calamity of the accident where she should have perished. Her suffering should have ended there and then. Instead, Karl Shadforth had resurrected the woman's brain and kept it functioning in a man-made dream. A cruel and demeaning existence for a brilliant mind.

The tears flowed freely for Cordelia as she sat before the frozen picture of a young and beautiful Rachelle Shaw on the monitor in front of her, as she was before she married, before she met...him, and before her children came along.

"So, so sorry, Rachelle. I never meant..."

"Bullshit! You were in on it from the beginning. You orchestrated the lie I lived through."

"No, not lived through. Manufactured only. You didn't live through any of it past the accident. That was all a part of the construct."

"Oh well, that makes it all right then. No harm, no foul, huh? Fuck you! I'm nothing more than a computer program. Probably even less than that. I don't even run the damn programs, do I?"

"You are so much more than that, Rachelle. You're a miracle."

"Shit! My children. Do they know...?"

"No, of course not. We..."

"Fuck that. You'd be capable of anything from where I'm

sitting...metaphorically speaking."

"Your children aren't old enough to know anything, Rachelle. You're conflating parts of the story with reality. Lorenzo is only a couple of years old. We couldn't tell them about you even if we'd wanted to. They are being cared for by a foster family."

"Why would you bother 'rescuing' me if all this shit is true? I can't believe any of this. All for what? A few stinking gems?"

"Those few stinking gems could change the financial future of our country, Rachelle. You know how economically unbalanced the world is at the moment with the energy crisis the way it is. It could mean the difference between surviving or not."

"And you think that justifies what you did to me? What you ARE doing to me?

"I don't, no. I never did. I was more or less forced into cooperating with Karl to come up with the psychology of the construct. He threatened my family and I had no choice."

"Your daughter?"

"No, that was part of the construct. My parents and siblings."

"So, where are we now and why did you do this? I would have been better off scrubbed out for good. This nightmare just keeps going."

"Would you like a chance to get back at him?"

"Just how the fuck would I do that? From inside a bloody computer?"

"What if there was a way for you to gain some form of physicality again?"

"I'm tired and I don't want to play twenty questions, so cut to the fucking chase, would you?"

"A former boyfriend of mine has been experimenting for years with robotics and cybernetics. He is very close to achieving a humanoid body structure that works reasonably well with a computer for a mind. What it requires, though, is a far more advanced mind and he hasn't cracked AI yet. It's the next logical step but he hasn't come even close to it in all the years of trying.

"When I mentioned the possibility of capturing a human consciousness within a computer, he immediately grasped the obvious. He saw a human mind as being capable of driving the artificial body, maybe even interacting or integrating with the computer presently contained in the body."

"You're joking, right?" asked Rizzo when the long pause stretched out.

"It's an idea. We don't know if it would work. You're the first of your kind, Rachelle."

"You want to put me inside an artificial body imitating a real person?"

"Ah, not exactly."

"What do you mean?"

"The body. Not very real looking, I'm afraid. Robot only. Metallic, with gears and gizmos. No covering," Cordelia winced with the information she was delivering, knowing how pathetic it was.

Sounds pretty cool!

"Fuck! You can't still be there. You're just a part of my imagination according to these creeps."

"No, I'm real, Rachelle..." Cordelia started.

"Not you! Rache, my younger self, in my head," explained Rizzo.

"That crept into your story somehow but was never a part of the construct. Karl remarked on that when you told him. I think it may be just part of a conscience thing, giving a personality to that side of ourselves that we argue with. You know, good and bad, that sort of thing?"

"No way. Bullshit! This is way beyond anything like that."

Too fucking right I am! Not going to explain me away with all that psychobabble crap.

"Rache is real. Real enough and I won't have her belittled by you."

"You might be suffering a form of split personality, Rachelle..."

"Stop it. I won't hear it. She's up there, in my mind and I won't have you trying to make her go away or explain away her existence."

"Okay, Rachelle, okay."

"And that's another thing. Call me Rizzo. She's Rache and I'm Rizzo."

"Well, this just became even weirder."

"One more thing."

"Really? There's more?"

"My memories, all of them. Is there any way of getting them back?"

"I have a copy of the deleted files but I don't have the coding experience to reintegrate them into the main file. My friend could possibly do it."

"Well, I'll agree to hear your friend out. That's as far as I'll commit. One thing, though... What's in it for you?"

"Besides doing the right thing? Revenge. I'd like to see Karl pay for what he's done to you, me and my family. If we get rich in the process that would be rather beneficial as well."

"Rich?"

"If we do make a plan to get even with him, it wouldn't hurt to explore that site you stumbled across before Karl has the chance to exploit it. I'd love to see him fail to get his mitts on those blue diamonds. There'll be no stopping him if he manages to find them first."

"That won't be a problem."

"What? Why wouldn't that be a problem?"

"The file I encrypted? It has the location of that site on it alright, but not the right one. There are multiple layers on that file. Code within code and that sequence of numbers I revealed only gave him access to the first layer of information which tells him nothing and indicates a dry creek bed, an old fossicking site my father and I used to frequent. My dad taught me very early on to cover my tracks completely when I'm fossicking. He'd learned that the hard way himself after getting ripped off by a supposed friend. He taught me how to secretly record the coordinates of a possible find within layers of code, and always leave a red herring in the first layer."

"Why commit the coordinates to hard copy in the first place? Why not memorise it?"

"Anything can happen to memory, as you damn-well know!"

"So Karl will find what if he goes to the site on the file?"

"Dirt, sand, a few useless rocks and maybe an agate or two. My dad and I used to love looking for agates."

"Wait, what about the plans for the laser drill?"

"What about them?"

"Are they real?"

"I won't know that for sure until I have my memories back."

TWENTY-ONE

"Rizzo? Rizzo, can you hear me?" asked a worried young man.

When Rizzo heard the words coming through, she wasn't sure where the sound was coming from. The quality of the words was very different from the sounds she'd been getting used to. They echoed to a certain degree. Gradually, she became aware of light filtering through to her. A light that became very bright. Too bright! She jerked!

"Sorry, sorry. My bad. Should've turned down the intensity on the penlight a bit. Um, nod if you can hear me."

Though Rizzo tried, she couldn't be sure if she managed to nod or not. She wasn't sure of anything at the moment. Her memories seemed to be clearing gradually...all of them as far as she could tell. That at least meant that something had gone right and that Steven had held up one part of the bargain. Truthfully, Rizzo was scared witless about what she would find out soon. It was one thing to be told about what would happen. Quite another to experience it in reality.

She hadn't been shown it. They were very reticent to reveal anything to her before she decided. The fact that she was thinking at all was a positive sign. They gave her no guarantees, only pathetic assurances of ground-breaking possibilities. It was infuriating to hear them discuss her as if she wasn't there listening to every word. So cold and calculating. Debating this and that about how to proceed, reciting endless lines of code while they attempted to integrate the neural pathways, connecting her mind to a...machine.

It should have been just another transfer of one set of programmes into another hardware housing. Only, the new housing would take time to adjust to her and vice versa. They said there was already a computer in the machine, a simple one capable of making the metal thing move awkwardly. Rizzo didn't know. She hadn't seen it in action.

A shutter suddenly opened wide to reveal a young man with worried features in front of her, attempting to shine his light into her 'eyes' once more. Rizzo managed to focus the lenses until the images before her coalesced into something approximating normal.

"Very good, Rizzo. I think your ocular lenses are working. Try to say something," suggested the handsome guy with long hair and geeky glasses.

Finding the pathways that allowed her to access the speaker took a few moments. The sound that came from it was anything but human or word-like. It pierced her senses and those of the man and woman in front of her, making them place their hands over their ears. The siren-like shriek was repeated as Rizzo tried again to say something.

"Whoa, let's do away with talking for the moment, shall we? I think you need some time with that one. Nod if you can hear and understand what I'm saying."

Rizzo managed a nod of the head. There was a certain cotton-like fuzziness to her thoughts, not at all clear and concise like she remembered them. The sounds she heard had a hollowness to them. Rizzo assumed it was because the receptors in her artificial ears were picking up the sound signals and relaying it to her in stereo. The inability to move and speak as she wanted was frustrating. There wasn't any indication of that for the benefit of her audience, as she had no means of communicating emotions.

There were going to be a great many limitations for her in the new body according to Steven and Cordelia. Most of the few weeks they had spent with Rizzo, were in preparation for the transfer and the repair of her memories. Then the day came for the transfer. She was warned that anything could happen, including non-functionality. That meant she could end, that her files could be irretrievably corrupted. No one could tell what the outcome would be.

Not for the first time did Rizzo wonder if she were simply being led through another construct, another manufactured reality to make her reveal the final layers of encryption. Who knew what was real anymore? Rache had been largely silent, not trusting of anyone or anything she witnessed. That was another conundrum. Was Rache real?

They explained that it could take many months for her to adapt to the body...the machine. It would be like learning to do everything over again, only far more complicated and awkward. The natural body knew automatically how to make limbs move and function without conscious effort. That wouldn't be possible for Rizzo. Nothing would come naturally and everything would require effort and training until it began to function semi-automatically.

"I imagine this is very difficult for you right now. Very strange. We'll take it slowly. Baby steps? It's okay, you don't have to answer. At the moment, your body is being supported by a standing cradle. It will take some time to train your body to respond to your commands. It will take time for your mind to search the neural pathways to operate the machinery. I can see the lenses for your eyes working, the aperture is opening and closing as you focus. See if you can nod your head a little to give me an indication that you understand what I'm saying."

It wasn't a nod per se, but the head moved a fraction. Rizzo admitted that she was scared. Petrified of what she would see once her body was revealed to her. She had specifically asked not to see it beforehand. It would have terrified her to see it and she doubted she would have had the courage to continue.

"Okay, excellent. So, we discussed this part, right? I'm going to move out of your line of sight to allow you to see the results in the mirror behind me. If I see your vital signs spiking, I'll shut you down immediately. If you panic, it burns out your electronic componentry. Try to be calm, Rizzo. Take your time and remain as calm as possible."

When Steven moved out of the way, Rizzo felt like she was holding her breath, which she knew wasn't possible. As prepared as she had been for the outcome, she froze when she finally saw...it.

Holy crap! You look like that killer robot from the old movie.

Rache was correct. It *was* almost like that robot. Shiny metal, glowing red lenses opening and closing of their own accord as the focus shifted up, down, side to side. Wires, cables, metal and gizmos approximating human limbs and musculature. The nightmare was complete for Rizzo. Going from a healthy female to a cripple living in an underground city, back to a young body and now...a machine. She didn't even have metal coverings like old C-3PO in the ancient movie. It was more like when Anakin Skywalker was still building the robot...exposing all the workings.

An innate sadness descended on Rizzo as she took in the ghastly sight. The head drooped visibly; the eyes downcast.

"I'm so sorry, Rizzo. It's not perfect, I know. I haven't had unlimited funds to work with. Everything I've done has been with a shoestring budget. If, if we find those gems, maybe we can do some upgrades. I've been experimenting with a polymer alloy that we might try to coat the body with. The trouble with that is, it has to be in sections that we can peel back or remove when we need to access parts."

The head rose slowly to turn towards, Steven. The head then turned sideways and back to indicate a negative to his suggestion.

"...Oooo."

Steven stared at the small speaker where a mouth would have been on a human, thinking he understood the word spoken to be a 'no'. There was no reason to make a normal mouth as no breath would be expelled to form actual vibrations in a larynx. Rizzo would have to learn to control the speech mechanism and the metallic voice coming through the speaker. It was a positive start despite the first negative reaction.

"...argh...ee..mm...me."

"I didn't get that." It's amazing that you're doing this so early, though. I didn't expect you to start talking for weeks."

"Mmm...ee. Me. Ssss...me....tay."

"This is you? This is how you want to stay? Did I get that right?"

A slight nod. Rizzo stared hard at the young man, then at Cordelia. Looking at the mirror once more, Rizzo felt the hard edge of her steely resolve returning. The monster had returned. The cripple with steel braces had been replaced by a full structure of titanium and super-aluminium alloy. The bitch inside the monster would perform the task the human could not manage. They would pay, they would all pay for what they had done to her.

TWENTY-TWO

The training proceeded with Rizzo making great strides in her development. Faster than Steven or Cordelia could have expected, Rizzo excelled in her capabilities with the body and speech. Although Cordelia, ever the psychoanalyst, had grave reservations about the mental aspects of Rizzo's personality, she applauded the speed with which the determined woman grasped the principles of taking over the functions of the body.

While Steven had suggested that Rizzo might eventually find a way of melding her programming with the simple computer onboard the body, it seemed to him that the melding had already occurred. Rizzo was taking milliseconds to make vast calculations and determinations during her lessons.

Steven watched closely as Rizzo began her run around the training field they had set up on a property on the Toowoomba Tablelands, far from prying eyes. Steven had inherited the property from his aunt a few years prior. He had always intended to create a laboratory for his work in the quiet surrounds nestled among native bushland on all sides. One hundred acres of virgin bush with only a small clearing in the centre to house the small rustic cabin.

Steven had borrowed a grader to construct an oval running track through the scrub around the clearing, measuring a kilometre in circumference. Cordelia and he sat stunned as they watched the dust cloud created by the heavy footfalls of the weighty robot making its tenth circuit of the track in record time.

"How are the vitals?" asked Steven.

"All good," answered Cordelia with her eyes glued to the tablet she held with all the readouts pertaining to the health and well-being of the robot. "Physically, she's mastering everything with astonishing speed.

"You still worried about her mental condition?"

"Not about concern for our safety, if that's what you mean?"

"Then?"

"She isn't the same. Her determination comes from another source that I don't see as healthy. I see signs of creeping darkness about her."

"Cut her some slack, Cord. She's been through it all. You saw to that."

"Jesus!"

Cordelia reared back as though she'd been slapped in the face.

"Sorry. That was uncalled for. Sorry, Cord. It's just that..."

"Yeah, I know. I feel guilty as hell for my part in all that. She says she doesn't hold it against me but..."

"Think she'll act out one day?"

"I think I have more to fear from Karl than her. He's not likely to be too pleased about finding nothing at those coordinates and he has serious backing from some heavy players."

"Safe enough here, no one knows where we are. Shit, look at that, she's just done the kilometre in under thirty seconds."

"She needs to slow it down. Battery needs charging."

"Let her go. Her early warning system will alert her. She needs this outlet for her mind. It's cleansing."

"Seems she got the alert. She's slowing. Here she comes."

"Broke your record again, Rizz," said Steven.

"What, Rizzo isn't short enough? You have to get shorter still?"

"Time for a recharge, Rizzo," said Cordelia quickly to ward off an argument.

"I am aware of that," answered Rizzo with her metallic voice making it difficult to know if she was angry or simply agreeing.

The monotone voice coming from the synthesiser would require some modulation to gain an approximation of emotions. Number one thousand two hundred and fifty-two on the 'to do' list. While the mechanics had held up reasonably well to the punishing regimen meted out by Rizzo, some parts needed maintenance regularly and others required replacements more often than Steven would have liked. Mechanical joints had shattered on many occasions when the body was being pushed to extreme limits.

Rizzo followed the others into the cabin in the centre of the small clearing. The charging point she used was located in the main living area, so Rizzo could partake in conversations or watch some TV while she remained plugged in. Charging generally required around three hours, during which she would have to power down most of her functions, to conserve the remaining power and reduce the time to recharge.

Steven and Cordelia were busy in the kitchen preparing their lunch while Rizzo turned on the TV as she made her way to the charging station. She froze mid-stride when she heard a community announcement being made over the local station. Unable to believe what she was hearing, she turned to face the screen. The pair stopped their lunch prep. Rizzo had frozen.

Viewing a red alert that appeared on the tablet she always carried, Cordelia became concerned when she saw the vital signs for Rizzo peaking alarmingly.

"Rizzo, what is it? You need to..."

"Did you know?" asked Rizzo in a tone that was unmistakably angry despite the limitations of the synthesiser.

"Know what?" asked Cordelia with surprise.

"How could you keep that from me? Why would..."

"Look, Rizzo, you're going critical and will shut down automatically if you don't lower the anxiety levels. You need to recharge and relax. I'll answer any questions you have then?"

Without answering her, Rizzo turned abruptly to make her way to the charging station. Once she reversed to where her back connected to the charging plate, she shut down most of her other functions. Waiting until she felt the revitalising charge entering her system and mentally calming herself, she glared back at Cordelia and Steven.

"What, what was it, Rizzo? What did you hear?"

"I heard a community announcement. A piano recital in the Toowoomba Community Hall. Tonight."

"What about it?" asked Steven with a feeling of dread.

"A piano recital by...Robert Rizzoli."

"You...you didn't know he survived?"

"Of course, I didn't know he bloody survived! I was told he died instantly. Broken neck. I saw..." breathed Rizzo with chilling clarity.

"You're mistaken about seeing it and you weren't told anything, Rizzo. You're confusing reality with the construct again. I am so sorry that I didn't think to tell you, Rizzo. It just..."

"Pretty big fucking omission, mate! How the fuck did that animal survive? The steering column went through his neck, didn't it?"

"Not possible, Rizzo."

"Oh? And why is that?"

"You were driving."

A deadly silence descended on the small living room with only the small electronic ticks coming from the charging station and the irises in Rizzo's lenses dilating open and shut with the tension.

"Care to run that by me again?"

"I thought you had all your memories back" Cordelia said quietly. "It's true, Rizzo. You were driving at the time of the accident. The black box indicates you took the vehicle off auto-drive and deliberately accelerated into the wall. The recordings of your argument before the crash were very clear. Robert threatened to take your children away from you, claiming he had unlimited funds to pay the best lawyers to accomplish that. You told him he would never get the children while you were alive. You disengaged the auto-drive, grabbed the wheel and drove straight into the wall. He survived. We thought you knew."

"Bullshit!" said Rizzo uncertainly. "You're fucking with me, right?"

"N-no, Rizzo. I wouldn't do that. It's the truth."

After several long moments, "I'm going."

"What? Going? Going where?"

"To the hall to see for myself."

"No, Rizzo, you can't."

"Who's going to stop me?"

The lenses narrowed to slits, into a stare that brooked no arguments or challenge. The cold steel of the featureless face stared at the two uncomprehending humans, baffled as to how they might stop the robot from revealing itself at a piano recital being attended by the good folk of Toowoomba. Automatons and industrial robots were commonplace in the 22nd century, however, Rizzo was far more advanced than anything the world had yet to experience.

Word of the visitation by a robot would make the headlines, eventually reaching the ears of Karl Shadforth. The connection would not be made immediately until the event was coupled to the name of the evening's performer; Robert Rizzoli. Karl was sure to conclude that Rizzo had been rescued. He was far too smart and suspicious not to put two and two together.

No amount of argument or common sense prevailed when Rizzo emerged from her charging session. Steadfastly refusing to listen to reason, Rizzo made preparations for the long trek into Toowoomba if they didn't agree to take her. Because of her immense weight, Rizzo could not be placed in a normal vehicle. Instead, it required her to be transported in the rear tray of a utility, or the back of a van.

The greatest fear for Cordelia and Steven was that Robert Rizzoli would not survive the evening, becoming the first victim of a robot murder and the riot it would produce. Knowing the way their patient felt, she was likely to rip him limb from limb without breaking into a sweat; not that she was able to sweat. A murder notwithstanding, there was also the problem of recognition to deal with. The general public was not about to take the presence of a robot watching the recital with good graces.

Cybernetics and artificial replacements were a hot topic of late with a huge outcry about using human parts on machines and vice versa. Prosthetics were no longer the harmless appendages they used to be. Humans, being what they were, had to use prosthetic or bionic limbs as an advantage in criminal activities or strongarming victims, bringing about much resentment among the non-enhanced populace.

Eventually, Rizzo accepted one compromise to alleviate their concerns regarding recognition. She was convinced to don a disguise. Wearing the niqab and burqa of a Muslim woman, Rizzo would not be seen as a robot unless closely inspected. The glowing red of the ocular lenses being the hardest to disguise. Behind the burqa, it allowed for a modicum of anonymity.

The trailing robes covered the metallic 'feet' of the robot as she made her way out of the van's side door, at the back of the community hall. Parking as far from the entrance or the lights as possible, Steven and Cordelia were visibly sweating despite the coolness of the evening air as they alighted. They were forced to don Muslim garb for themselves as well, to fit in with their charge, though Cordelia opted for the hijab over the full burqa. The tension was palpable.

Rizzo had not uttered one word during the drive into Toowoomba. They dreaded the evening to come, knowing full-well the inevitable outcome. Unbeknownst to Rizzo, Steven carried with him an electronic object of similar dimensions to a TV remote control. He fervently hoped he would not have to resort to using the device. There would be limited opportunities to deploy it, so the timing would be of the essence. He wondered if he was up to the task.

Most of the gathering had entered the hall ahead of the late-comers arriving in the non-descript white van with the sagging back axle. The trio of unusually-clad patrons entered the rear of the hall to sit in the last row of wooden benches. The stage lights flickered.

A single spotlight illuminated the floorboards, bare but for the grand piano resting centre stage. Polite applause broke out as a tall, elegant man in traditional tails entered from stage left. With a limp, he took his position on the stool in front of the piano. The atrium lights dimmed further. Had she a heart, it would have thudded in Rizzo's chest at that moment.

From the first delicate note to the crashing last, the crowd were enthralled. Rizzo swivelled her head to watch the audience members around her with interest. The audience was silent. Any break in the music would allow for a pin drop to be heard as the maestro played on the stage. From the pianissimo to the forte, the grandeur of the movements and the sweet notes of the chords coursed through the chamber with exquisite acoustic clarity.

Rizzo watched in silent awe as the tears among the female patrons and more than one male flowed freely. The music moved her. The playing was superb, sensitive and so unlike anything she remembered of the monster that he was. She had never heard him playing anything but head-banging techno-rock. She did not recognise the calm and cultured man at the piano on the stage in front of her. He was lost in his world of pure music. She could identify immediately the pure love and passion he exhibited for the mellifluous notes he played.

Once again, she lowered her head as an innate sadness overtook her. It was true, she had forced him to become the monster she knew. He changed because she had become pregnant and more or less forced him to extend the record label contract and play with the band for longer than he wanted. Rachelle Shaw had taken away the man's dreams and shattered his perceived future. She had laid down the law of responsibility on him with another man's children and crushed his hopes in the process. What she saw before her was the real man. Had she recognised that at the time, he would not, in all likelihood, have taken to drinking or drugs.

Nothing was certain but it seemed clear to Rizzo. He felt

trapped by the constraints of marriage and impending fatherhood to someone else's children. Gone was the carefree man with the sole ambition to attend the Academy of Music in Adelaide. Born was the troubled man who'd lost everything he'd trained for. Money wasn't a problem with the record label signing the band. In his eyes, the real problem was the life he had to abandon. He hated the techno scene even though he was brilliant at it. Rizzo saw then that he could have been brilliant at any music he chose, such was his innate talent. But he had only one style of music that he lived for and longed to play for the rest of his years.

Long after the recital had concluded to a standing ovation with several encores, did Rizzo remain cemented to her seat at the rear of the auditorium. The audience had filed past with the occasional glance thrown the way of the silent trio sitting in the back. At one point, both Cordelia and Steven wondered if she had powered down, she had been that still. They grew alarmed when a man came limping onto the stage to collect his music from the piano and Rizzo rose to walk down the centre aisle. Steven's hand went immediately to the device in his trouser pocket, yet stayed his fingers at Cordelia's touch.

Robert Rizzoli looked up when he heard the heavy footsteps approaching. Shielding his eyes from the bright lights directed at the stage, he watched as the unusual trio of persons approached. One large woman covered from head to toe in robes and a burqa stopped by the apron of the stage. He watched with curiosity as the large woman bent down to whisper to the other woman.

"My sister would like to warn you about her voice before she speaks to you. She had an injury that left her with a damaged larynx and speaks through a synthesiser," explained Cordelia.

"I see. Well, thank you for the warning, though I'm sure it wouldn't have alarmed me. What can I do for you?"

"I would just like to thank you for the most enlightening and uplifting performance I have ever had the privilege of experiencing. You are an artist of unparalleled skill in the modern era. I wanted you to know how very much you have touched me tonight. I hope you can find it in your heart to forgive me...for everything," said Rizzo as she turned immediately to stride back the way she came, leaving Robert scratching his head.

Cordelia and Steven respected her silent introspection on the return journey. Rizzo sat on the single seat in the rear of the otherwise empty van contemplating the truths and the lies of her life as told by others and even herself. For she *had* lied to herself. She excluded many facts from her life with Robert Rizzoli. She had deliberately obfuscated many of the scenes in her memories to make herself out to be the hapless victim. The truth saddened her deeply.

The silence continued through the night as Rizzo marched through the cabin to stand at her charging station in sleep mode. In reality, Rizzo was scanning the internet through her neural connections, finding every piece of information possible about her ex-husband. He'd spent some months in hospital according to the newscasts, recovering from a smashed knee. The record label had reneged on a second album deal, leaving Robert Rizzoli, still a wealthy man. but with no band or future in the techno-rock industry.

With Robert unable to rehearse and losing all interest in the band, they went their separate ways after a brief and illustrious career. It seemed Robert became somewhat of a recluse after announcing his drug and alcohol habit to the media and disappearing into some rehab centre. Rizzo found where he had attended the audition for the Academy and gained entry.

Abandoned by his regular fans, Robert slowly gained critical acclaim as a pianist while attending the Academy. Hailed as an upcoming virtuoso, Robert also became well-known for his compositions, with comparisons being made to the sublime skill of Rachmaninov coupled with the sensitivity of a Camille Saint-Saëns. His star was gradually rising and Robert appeared to be a happy and content man, regularly attending local AA meetings. His pronounced limp was the only physical reminder of the horrific crash.

Rizzo could find no information about her children no matter how deeply she penetrated the web. She used the following weeks to gather everything available regarding robotics, linguistic programs, and any other pertinent information to her situation. While it appeared to Cordelia and Steven as though Rizzo had retreated into a mental breakdown, the opposite was true.

She was gaining information with a speed that rivalled the expectations of her hosts. She began to reprogram her complex coding with her original script, her variation. Her computational skills increased exponentially; her software exceeded known parameters in all areas of functionality.

Steven and Cordelia watched on silently as Rizzo began a series of mechanical upgrades, the likes of which had them gasping in awe. Creating a new plastic-alloy compound, they observed the robot become more human-like in appearance every day, though still chrome. Steven closely observed while Rizzo replaced the speaker mechanism with a working set of jaws that closely approximated a human's. He was unable to follow the process as closely as he would have liked for the speed at which it was performed.

While remaining androgynous, the new covering gave her a softer appearance, though metallic silver in colour. Six months after the recital, Rizzo spoke for the first time, in a clear voice devoid of the former artificial tones.

"A patent has been filed for a laser drill by Dr Thoms. Testing of the prototype is to commence at an undisclosed site in the coming days. We have to find them and stop the test," said Rizzo to the stunned pair standing before her.

"You've done a marvellous job with that voice. How..."

"Forget that, Steven. We have a major problem."

"What is it, Rizzo?" asked Cordelia.

"Evidently, Karl decided to make a fortune out of tapping geothermal pockets for energy when he didn't find the blue diamonds. He gave my designs in that file to Dr Thoms."

"Yes, you said the designs were in the file. What's the problem?"

"Now that I have my full memories back, I know I also concealed the complete designs for the drill under layers of protection like the site of the diamonds. If Dr Thoms followed my designs faithfully, he is about to unleash exactly what we hoped to avoid, depending on where he hopes to test the drill."

"I don't like the sound of that. Are you sure?"

"Not certain, no. There is a flaw, a fatal flaw, in the design in that first file layer. If no one picked up on it, it has the potential to do exactly what that story of yours revealed."

"No, Rizzo. It was all make-believe. Sure, we used basic truths to build upon, like coming up with a drill and so on. Attributing that to Dr Thoms instead of you but none of it was real. It was purely a construct we built to get you to release the information on the encryption."

"You don't believe what I'm telling you?"

"We believe that you believe."

"What sort of horseshit is that? Psycho-babble to amuse me, to placate me? I'm telling you I protected my design with an intentional flaw in case anyone managed to break through my first layer of protection, just like I gave a false site for the sample I sent off to have analysed. If he fires off that laser drill with the design they have, they will unleash a chain reaction. Don't you understand, it can corrupt the core?"

"Why would you do that? Why would you deliberately include such a catastrophic flaw in your design, knowing what could eventuate?"

"Let's put it down to being young, arrogant and selfish. If someone ended up stealing my design, I was going to make sure they paid. I've realised lately that my ex-husband wasn't the real monster I made him out to be. I've woken up to a great many truths of late and I'm not liking what I'm seeing at all."

"How did you find out about the patent?"

"Same way I've been doing these upgrades. By searching the web using flags I'd coded in. Sorry, Steven, but your designs are way out of date since I've been in charge of my body. My brain is also integrated with the computer I've been enhancing and upgrading all this time. I've recoded everything with my new coding language. I'll happily give it to you, everything I've done after we achieve what we have to do. We have to stop Karl and Henry Thoms from testing the drill. After that, it's all yours. The diamonds, if there are any, are yours too. The drill with the proper specs and the new computer code with all the schematics for true AI. You two will probably be the richest people on earth with all that. I only ask one thing in return."

"Which is?"

"You find my children and set up a legacy so that they will never want for anything during their lives. Protect them."

"Why wouldn't you...?"

"NO! They will never see me like this. I couldn't do that to them. They're better off believing I'm dead. It has to stay that way."

"I don't know what to say," admitted Cordelia.

"Will you do it?"

"Of course. Will the drill test do as much damage as you say?"

"Without the correction, the laser will not fire in the Gatling gun sequence of short powerful bursts. Instead, the laser will fire on all points in one sustained burst capable of reaching practically through the earth. If they give it the power I recommended in my notes, the effects will be catastrophic. The domino effect on the world's lithospheric plates and volcanoes will be unavoidable and devastating. Your story wasn't at all far-fetched compared to the reality of the doomsday device I created. Me, Rachelle Rizzoli, world-ender. Any ideas as to where Karl and Henry might go to test the drill?"

"He does have a drilling platform."

"An underwater platform?"

"No, above water. An oil exploration rig in the process of being carted out beyond the three-mile limit," explained Cordelia.

"Tell me it isn't going anywhere near the Bougainville Trench."

"I don't know where it was headed. I heard talk of a joint venture between his company and the government of the Solomon Islands," she ventured.

"How did I miss that in my searches?"

"He covers his tracks well with offshore shell companies and a paper trail nobody could connect to him. I only knew about a small part of his dealings and that was massive. All very hush-hush and skirting legality."

"Can you give me a list of what you know? I'll use that to try and uncover the rest. I don't think we have much time."

TWENTY-THREE

Rizzo had made striking advancements on her physiognomy as the weeks progressed. Still a spectacularly polished chrome edifice, she now sported moulded glass eyes with only a slight reddish tinge in a face that had defined cheekbones and lips. A nicely shaped bald cranium topped off the slimmed-down, smooth chrome body. Her strength, agility and speed were breathtaking to the observers.

Her ability to charge while in full functioning mode, using all available natural resources like sun, wind, and the Earth's magnetic field meant that she no longer required a charging station or downtime. It was a constant process that kept her fully charged at all times no matter how much was being expended in energy. Most rigid mechanical parts had been replaced with flexible components that baffled Steven as he watched the process. When he caught a glimpse of the coding she used to upgrade her software, he was unable to make heads or tails out of it.

Rizzo had scoured the web to determine the position of the drilling platform, piggy-backing off satellites and bouncing back off cell towers and dishes. Narrowing in on the platform's position finally came one afternoon while Rizzo was viewing a military satellite's imagery. Karl and his company had opted for a land-based drilling platform situated near Mt Gambier in South Australia.

"He's going to access the dormant magma basin under Mt Gambier, last thought to have erupted only 5,000 years ago. It will set off the volcanic chain that exists there with Mt Schank being its next explosive neighbour. There are nearly four hundred dormant and extinct volcanoes along a 2,000klm stretch of the southeast coast of Australia, all of which will be in danger of erupting if he succeeds," announced Rizzo. Steven and Cordelia sat in silence, stunned.

TWENTY-FOUR

A lone figure of chrome stood beside a small lake in South Australia situated one hundred kilometres from Mt Gambier. The afternoon sky glowed a brilliant red, bathing the entire scene in an ethereal crimson wash. On the horizon, the column of ash spewing from the top of the mountain reached tens of kilometres into the sky. The ground beneath shook violently causing ripples across the smooth glass water of the lake, having reflected the tumultuous sky only seconds before.

The glassy, unblinking eyes peered solemnly at the portentous vista. Though there were no emotions visible on the smooth metallic face, anyone observing the figure could guess at the sadness from the stillness and the way the head tilted downward after a time. They were too late. Rizzo had found the drilling site too late for them to prevent the test.

The two humans standing behind the robot watched in fear as the apocalypse began. They had ringside seats to the end of the world and the one responsible stood a few metres away.

"You said the story was a fabrication. How is this happening like it did in that story? Why did you put that stuff in the construct about the flaw in the drill?" asked Rizzo in a perfectly formed voice devoid of any artificial sound.

"I came up with the basic infrastructure for the story, but a lot of it was fuelled by you, your experiences, memories and possible dreams. We had to improvise on the fly at all times to keep up with the narrative that you added. The booby-trap you set in the file in real life must have prompted you to come up with a flaw in the drill design which you then ascribed to Dr Thoms in the story."

"It's all coming true. Me. I did this! I am a true monster inside and out, all the way to the bitter end. Only there won't be an end for me, will there? I'll get to watch everyone else perish one way or another while I outlast them all. I made sure of that with all the upgrades. My batteries are built to last forever. Nano-bots inside me automatically repair and replace everything that wears out or breaks. Everything inside me can be manufactured from scratch by microscopic bots. It will all die and I'll possibly be the only one left to witness it. Only one small consolation to all this, I get to see the end of them. Thoms the rapist and Shadforth the evil prick. They would have been there at the site."

"How long, Rizzo?" asked Steven in a shaky voice.

"A year or two before the air becomes unbreathable and the ash cloud envelops the Earth."

"Will it get to that, are you sure?"

"This is only the first of the eruptions and quakes. It'll trigger others. I suspect that the Pacific Ring of Fire will be impacted, just as in the story you fabricated. Once that starts, the tsunamis will wipe out much of the eastern seaboard. All the Pacific islands will be toast. It'll start a volcanic winter that will wipe out all animal and human life as we know it. A few unlucky souls will make it to underground bunkers. They'll have to stay down there for the rest of their lives and possibly generations to come if they last that long. Not very likely. Unless..."

"Unless" ventured Cordelia.

"Unless we follow some of my story to build that ark. A bank of embryos in stasis for when the world recovers. Embryos of the animals and humans, all cared for by a robot capable of lasting the distance. Capable of waiting the required time for the earth to heal. Capable of caring for the bank of embryos until that time, underground or above, because the robot doesn't require air to continue. A very small gesture of compensation to assuage the guilt of the one responsible. Would there be a pair of humans willing to assist a robot and her living conscience to achieve that goal, I wonder?"

"Rizzo?"

"Want to help me save humankind from extinction?"

I'm in.

To Be Continued...

ABOUT THE AUTHOR

Josef (Joe), came to Australia with his parents and two siblings in 1964, leaving an ailing and broken Germany behind. A lack of confidence stemming from a poor education meant that Joe's passion for writing never gained traction until his later years. He now lives in the small country NSW town of Moulamein, where he owns and runs a caravan park with his wife. He writes purely to entertain his audiences and himself with true-blue Aussie tales located in a country he loves deeply.